PRAISE FOR
Sherlock in Love

"A surprisingly moving mystery that's also one of the most believable Holmes and Watson spinoffs ever. . . . Most haunting [is] the story of old Dr. Watson trying to restore his dear friend Holmes to life by writing about him. By the end of *Sherlock in Love* even the most skeptical of Naslund's readers will believe such miracles can happen. . . . Dazzling." —National Public Radio

"A triumphant reimagining of the Sherlock Holmes canon that identifies, once and for all, the great love of the detective's life. . . . One of the very few Holmes pastiches that not only honors the great man's memory but unleashes his residual mythic power for more ambitious purposes." —*Kirkus Reviews*

"Original and affecting. . . . Naslund has constructed an intricate plot . . . unusually poignant." —*Los Angeles Times*

"Loaded with surprises and twists of plot appropriate to Sherlock Holmes. Irresistible." —*The State* (Columbia, SC)

"Cleverly plotted. . . . Naslund's historical references are entertaining, while her dramatization of sexual tension and doomed romance shows us facets of Holmes we've never seen before." —*Booklist*

"Entertains at breakneck speed." —*New York Times*

"A treasure of a book. . . . For many of us who have been waiting for a wonderful Sherlock Holmes adventure, true to the spirit of the original stories and worthy of them, Sena Jeter Naslund's *Sherlock in Love* is the most welcome and captivating of gifts." —*Courier-Journal* (Louisville, KY)

Sherlock in Love

ALSO BY SENA JETER NASLUND

The Disobedience of Water

Ahab's Wife

Sherlock
❧ in ❧
Love

A NOVEL BY
SENA JETER NASLUND

Perennial
An Imprint of HarperCollinsPublishers

The author acknowledges support from the National Endowment for the Arts, the Kentucky Arts Council, the Kentucky Foundation for Women and the Lawrence Fiction Prize.

This book was originally published in 1993 by David R. Godine, Publisher, Inc.

HarperCollins books may be purchased for educational, business, or sales promotional use. For information please write: Special Markets Department, HarperCollins Publishers Inc., 10 East 53rd Street, New York, NY 10022.

First Perennial edition published 2001.

The Library of Congress has catalogued the hardcover edition as follows:

Naslund, Sena Jeter.
Sherlock in love: a novel/by Sena Jeter Naslund.—I st ed.
p. cm
ISBN 0–87923–977–8
I. Holmes, Sherlock (Fictitous character)—Fiction. 2. Private investigators—England—Fiction. I. Title
PS3564.A827S48 1993 813' .54–dc20 93–28449 CIP

ISBN 0-688-17844-8 (pbk.)

01 02 03 04 05 RRD 10 9 8 7 6 5 4 3 2 1

To

Karen J. Mann

and for

Flora

ACKNOWLEDGMENTS

An encouraging word at a crucial moment from my painter friend Corie Rouse Neumayer made it possible for me to begin this book. I also wish to thank Linda Beattie, Marcia Woodruff Dalton, Rob LaFreniere, Robin Lippincott, Maureen Morehead, Alan Naslund, Rick Neumayer, Bill Pearce, Jonathan Penner, Deborah and David Stewart, Janet Streepey, Daly Walker, and Luke Wallin.

I am grateful to Lucinda Sullivan, whose comments on the book transformed it; Roger Weingarten, director of the MFA in Writing at Vermont College, without whose active support and faith this work would not be in its present form; Mark Polizzotti, my invaluable editor.

The person who made this book happen, finally, through her sustaining enthusiasm, her insights, and indefatigable work with me in revising, is Karen J. Mann, and it is to her that I dedicate *Sherlock in Love*. And to my daughter Flora, who at age ten when I read her a chapter of the novel, said, with shining eyes, "More!"

CONTENTS

I

THE
PRESENT

❧ I ❧

SILHOUETTE

Holmes was dead: to begin with. And had been dead for well onto two years. And who was I without Holmes? He had been my dearest friend. He had served as that fixed point around which my life as a storyteller revolved.

Sometimes, on dreary December days such as this one, when the fog was so thick over London one could scarcely tell whether it was woman or man who hurried by in the street, I would think that I had seen him. When Holmes seemed to brush by me in the gloom, I could not refrain from hastening my aged legs and ignoring my ancient wound from Afghanistan in order to overtake the figure. Then in the cone of light falling from some street lamp, the veils of obscuring mist would be turned back and there would stand, perhaps, some sharp-nosed woman, dressed in the wretched modern coat and boots, loaded with Christmas packages.

The idea of Holmes had teased my vision so much that I had determined to take up my pen, to exorcise the ghost by writing about him again. Not an isolated adventure, but a definitive biography. On the first day of winter, December 21, 1922, my advertisement appeared in the *Times:*

THE BIOGRAPHY OF SHERLOCK HOLMES TO
BE WRITTEN. HIS CHRONICLER REQUESTS
INTERVIEWS, LETTERS, ETC. CONCERNING
HIM. CONTACT JOHN WATSON M.D., 221B
BAKER STREET.

I hoped that I yet possessed a head clear enough for the task. Fogged by grief and loneliness (the last Mrs. Watson had died years before Holmes), my memory had become uncertain. Even the various Adventures that I had penned were a whirl of places and people, many long since deceased.

Not wishing to spend the day alone at Baker Street, waiting for replies and fidgeting, I had stayed in the British Museum till nightfall. As I hurried home, a terrible wind blew the fog about and made my arms seem thin and unprotected inside my greatcoat. The winter wind howled as though it were alone and weary of this world.

When a large dog sauntered out of a doorway, I started, envisioning that ghastly hound who had haunted the last of the Baskervilles until Holmes and I had ended its career on just such a gloomy night as this. But perceiving on second sight that this beast was of a more kindly disposition, I spoke and tried to snap my fingers through my thick leather gloves. "Here, fellow," I said. His breath and mine caused even denser balloons of mist to surround our heads. A door opened and the face of a man topped with violent red hair protruded. "You wouldn't be trying to pinch me dog, would you?" he said.

Embarrassed, I hurried on against the fierce wind toward the old Baker Street apartment. I would read again of the grand old pursuits, and I was eager for the warmth of our familiar lodgings. Soon after the last Mrs. Watson died, Holmes had left off beekeeping down in Sussex and had invited me to return with him to Baker Street.

A light that I had left on for myself shone through one of the three slender and arched windows. And there, on the other side of the drawn shade, wearing his Inverness and deerstalker, passed the shadow of Sherlock Holmes.

"Holmes!" I shouted, "Holmes!" more glad-hearted than terrified, for there, it seemed, he stood, silhouetted in the window above me. Once before I had thought him dead, in the falls of Reichenbach, and he had returned. The silhouette stooped and lifted—the violin! As he tucked it under his chin, I charged the door.

I thrust first one key, the wrong one, and then another into the lock. I threw open the door and dashed as though winged through the hall and up the stairs. "Holmes," I cried, and felt as nimble as I had rushing the enemy line in Afghanistan, though I could hear my own hoarse breath like a kind of croaking.

As I ran, the frail voice of Mrs. Hudson, blind now and confined to a wheelchair, called, "It's he!" Naturally, I supposed it was the great detective to whom she referred. "It's he!" The words spurred me on. I flung myself through the door, knowing I would now see Holmes standing in the lamplight. But alas, the lamp burned in solitude. There was no sign of Holmes. The closed violin case lay as usual on the table beside the lamp.

I confess that I sank into one of the armchairs beside the fireplace and wept. My dizzy ascent thundered in my head.

Mary, our housemaid, stood in the door and said, "Mrs. 'Udson's quite 'urt, begging your pardon, sir, that you didn't stop to greet her. She recognizes your footstep, you know, sir."

"Yes, I'll be down," I said dully. Of course it had been my own energetic footstep the old woman had triumphantly acknowledged. But oh, the difference between this miserable practitioner and that great cold intellect who once inhabited these rooms. I waved the girl away.

Now, I said to myself, things are going too far. Anyone might mistake a shape or two at night in a winter street, but one must not allow oneself to go charging up stairs after beings who could exist only in one's own mind. Sure to induce heart failure, I severely told myself, in a man of my extreme age. I recalled how the old pump had worked. Very well, after all. After all, perhaps not the worst way to go.

Feeling hot, I threw my coat open and walked slowly to the mantel. I took down the Persian slipper in which Holmes had always housed his shag. In fact, I kept a bit of the tobacco there myself now. I buried my nose in the toe of the slipper to have a comforting whiff.

But the shadow had moved! He had tucked the violin under his chin; I had seen the angle of the arm, bent at the elbow, supporting the instrument.

"Holmes?" I called out. Silence. More loudly: *"Holmes?"*

But the spirit could not be recalled. I felt like a child in a schoolroom where no companion lingered.

As Holmes had said about that supposedly supernatural hound, we must not turn to the other world for explanations till those in this world have been exhausted. Probably some piece of furniture had thrown a deceiving shadow across the window shade. But, no object cast a Holmes-like shadow now. All was in order.

One must not make assumptions. One must observe. Since entering the room, I had not touched the light. If I returned to the street, I should again be able to observe the shadow. My body groaned at the idea of going down and up the steps again. But, if I ever did meet Holmes in the afterworld, I shouldn't want him to look at me scornfully. *A flight of stairs, Watson,* he might say, *kept you from learning the facts?* No. It wouldn't do.

Remembering the bitter weather of the street, I buttoned my coat again. I walked wearily to the center window of the three and shoved aside the curtain. Perhaps the night was not so dark, so cold, so blown with fog as I had recently experienced. But there—lounging across the street! My body stiffened for action. The figure moved, and then I saw clearly that it was only a woman dressed all in red. The Woman in Red—I had written about such a woman long ago. Could I recall her name? Yes—Irene Adler. Irrelevant, I told myself angrily. Go down into the street and see which hat rack in this room has come to resemble your late friend.

Slowly I crossed the worn carpet. Once it had been heavily patterned in a dark red floral design. Now the dun-coloured jute threads were all that was left in many places. Well, when I got back I would have some brandy.

I quietly descended to the ground floor, slipping successfully past Mrs. Hudson's door and out onto the pavement. Once below, I sought out my former position and lifted my eyes eagerly to the first floor. There was no shadow. The window was a blank of light. I waited some minutes, but as there was absolutely no variation, I deemed any further vigil to be fruitless. I resolved again simply to forget the matter.

This time I made no attempt to keep my presence unknown to Mrs. Hudson, but neither she nor Mary hailed me. I thought that it was perhaps a bit mean of me not to greet the ladies, who were doubtlessly lonely. Mrs. Hudson was probably dozing, or she would have called out to Mary that it was I, on hearing my footstep. I knocked courteously.

Mary opened the door; Mrs. Hudson was not at all asleep. She sat beside a tiny green Christmas tree ablaze with miniature wax candles.

"A Merry Christmas to you, Mrs. Hudson," I said, trying to sound jovial. "If you could only see your tree. It's quite beautiful."

"I feel it, Dr. Watson. I feel the warmth."

"And she's got them bells, too, sir," Mary put in. "Excuse me, there's a footstep in the 'all."

Mrs. Hudson beckoned to me, and when I had come close enough to suit her she said, "Listen," and she took up one of three little round-topped bells sitting on the mahogany table near the tree. Holding it close to her ear, she rang the bell: the sweetest little ding-ding, and for some reason it made tears start to my eyes.

"I'm afraid I must go up," I said. "I'm quite fatigued."

Mary reappeared, "Did you ring for me?"

"Who was it, Mary?" Mrs. Hudson tilted up her blind face.

"Just the wind," Mary answered, puzzled.

"By the way, Dr. Watson, you have some mail," Mrs. Hudson told me. "Mary, give Dr. Watson his letter."

Mary scurried to the sideboard and retrieved a small, buff-coloured envelope.

I gave Mary a coin, wished her the joy of the season, and took my leave. The candles fluttered like little birds in the tree.

I dragged my heavy body up the stairs. As I entered the sitting room, the black case of the violin drew me toward it. Idly, I snapped open the bright locks. Rosin dust still powdered the wood around the bridge. I picked up the violin. What a slender neck! How Holmes had loved to play! The plush purple interior of the case was fitted out with a number of little compartments for housing extra strings, rosin, a dustcloth. When I lifted the dustcloth I found a piece of paper—a note. It was jagged at the bottom, something torn off. I read:

June 12, 1886

Dear Holmes,

Should you have travelled after me to Berg, this note will serve to bid you farewell. I feel that I am no less doomed than the King, and indeed, I half desire to die.

I should very much like for you to have the

Stradivarius violin which I purchased in London.
I have sent it to the address noted below.
To you and Dr. Watson, I wish the happiness of
a life that I was not destined to share.
V. Sigerson

Rather presumptuous fellow, Victor Sigerson. How could he possibly have shared a life with Holmes and me?

Sigerson? Yes, I remembered him. Quite a good fiddler. And he had left Holmes this violin. I supposed that was why Holmes used the name Sigerson occasionally when he played in pubs. Some adventure was connected with Sigerson. Dead now, too. I supposed it would be in my notes some place. One of the unpublished Adventures.

Sigerson. I felt sad when his name echoed in my mind. I poured myself a brandy and reflected. What had Holmes thought of the fellow? Quite a gift—a Stradivarius. We must have done something rather significant for him. I couldn't remember. When I compiled the details for the biography, I would look for Sigerson.

Why not begin at once? Biographical research could commence! I went straight to the breakfront bookcase. There on the lowest shelves stood the rows of Holmes's tall commonplace books. Each was neatly lettered on its buckram spine in his own hand. I went right about the business and pulled out the S volume. I thumbed to Si and on to Sig.

But here occurred a gap.

I turned up the gas and got out the magnifying lens. An inspection of the binding showed that someone, probably using a sharp razor, had excised several pages. Indeed, the stitches of the entire volume had been rendered insecure by the operation, and the surrounding pages wobbled in the binding like loose teeth.

When did that happen? Was it Holmes himself who had cut out the pages? What could he have written there about Sigerson?

Or had someone been in my apartment! Holmes's own silhouette appeared in my memory, and I shuddered. London fog seemed to sweep through my mind. Surely the shade of Holmes had been a mere projection, and yet someone had cut pages from this book. Sometime.

I took out my rule and measured and recorded the exact size of the pages of the commonplace book. This way if I were to run upon the missing pages, having my rule with me, I could measure them and ascertain if they were the authentic size. Recognition cannot be left to mere resemblance, as any bibliophile will attest.

I reached for my snifter and thought, quite inappropriately, *Suppose you should die tonight?* Outrageous idea! Why tonight over any other night? And yet, I thought, if I *were* to leave these rooms, what would be a better wharf from which to untie, so to speak, than Holmes's bed?

Without further ado, I collected my nightclothes, went into Holmes's room and readied myself for sleep. Soon I was turning back the covers of a bed that had not been slept in for two years.

My head felt chilly, and I reached under the pillow hoping that I would find Holmes's old nightcap. For a moment my fingertips touched only the cold smooth linen. Were even the material objects associated with Holmes destined to vanish? My fingers groped further in that icy place and then brushed against the comfortable texture of flannel. I quickly put on the cap, and I must have fallen asleep almost at once.

When I awoke I was utterly astonished to see moving toward me across the dark bedroom, a small tree of flickering lights. It had an unearthly glow, soft and gentle. Not a fearsome thing, but wondrously strange. And then I saw that the tree had little feet bound in old-fashioned button-boots—ladies' boots—and what appeared to be the tree was actually the skirt of a full, green apron, wreathed round and round by tiny pockets, each with a candle in it. And, indeed the Christmas tree was Mrs. Hudson, standing up with her eyes shining, as though she were not crippled and blind.

"Remember your mail," she said in quite her natural voice.

I jumped out of bed. My single candle was still burning beside my half-empty glass. What phenomenon had that been? A dream, of course, I told myself.

It was true I had not opened the mail. At this rate, research for the biography would proceed at the speed of glaciation. I took up my candle and lighted my way to the sitting room.

Turning up the gas, I saw I had carelessly left the letter on the acid-stained, deal-topped table, the one Holmes had kept in the corner for his chemical experiments.

I tore open the envelope. It would *not* be a letter from Holmes, I told myself with good humour. My spectacles were not to be found, so I took out Holmes's old magnifying lens. How he used to lie stretched out full-length on the ground peering at footprints! A ludicrous posture, I always thought. The letter:

Dr. Watson,

Beware the ghost of Sherlock Holmes. Take measures to protect your life.

I repeat: guard your life. Secure your lodgings, or you will not live to see the New Year.

Announce in the Times that you have abandoned the project.

A Friend
(Who seeks to protect you)

Gradually my amazement was replaced with irritation. What was this? A threat? A warning? The biography would bring focus to my mind and give me purpose again.

Who can call himself a friend but refuse to sign his name? I had no need for such a "protector." Probably a minor criminal whom Holmes had put away. Possibly rehabilitated, and not wishing his name to appear in the biography.

I threw the note into the fire and watched the edges blacken, curl, and then burst into flame. I returned to bed.

As I dozed off, my toes feeling quite cold, I heard, I thought, the soft ding of a silver bell. It seemed very near, almost at my ear. Only two little shivers of a sound. Beware, *beware.*

2

A FIGURE EMERGES
FROM THE PAST

I WOULD HAVE forgotten the ghost of Sherlock Holmes, but a second visitation occurred.

The next night when it was pitch black on Baker Street, a blast of wind vibrated the window glass of my rooms, and I glanced out to see a newspaper tumbling through the dark street. The paper made fantastic swoops and turns, rose almost to the height of the doors. In one doorway stood an old woman with a mongrel dog pulling on her skirt. It was an odd sight. The dog seemed not at all vicious but somehow solicitous—as though he cared for this woman and wanted her to go with him. Her skirt was long, old-fashioned, and somber. As I watched them the woman raised her face toward my window. Upon seeing me she jumped, pulled her skirt away from the dog, and began to shuffle off down the street.

The dog trotted after her willingly enough but occasionally circled in front of her as though he wished for her to turn around. I hated to see an old woman so alone and in the cold; last night there had been a woman in red lounging across the street. Now the wind wrapped the dark skirt about the legs of this woman, and her dog clamped his tail low between his legs. Why had *I* startled her from her haven in the doorway?

After they turned a corner out of sight, I detected another stranger—a solitary man—coming into view. He wore a bowler, much like my own favoured headpiece, and because of the high wind, he was obliged to walk with his hand securing his hat to his head. He wore a greatcoat, and a bit of a muffler, like the tail of a kite, blew around him. He took very long strides, and he seemed to glance at the house numbers on my side of the street as he progressed toward me. He walked like a man who had been walking all day. How many times had Holmes and I, in an idle moment, stood here at the window and watched the passers-by! Often Holmes could spot a person whose hurried or anxious manner, whose checking of some address-card against the numbers, suggested that he would soon present himself as a client.

My night-walker glanced up at me and started as though he had seen a spectre. He rushed to the door, and within an instant I heard him ringing below, and then came Mary with a query as to whether it was not too late this evening for me to receive a caller.

Hurriedly, I brushed off the visitor's chair. I grabbed the nearest pipe, lit up, and seated myself in Holmes's chair. Surely no emissary of death would present himself so forthrightly.

When the man entered, I noted that he was about forty-five, tall, as I had observed by the length of his stride.

His face was well-lined, though he had something of a jaunty expression. I surmised that he had been out in the weather a good deal or that he had laboured under many cares, or both.

"Dr. Watson," he greeted me, holding out his hand. "Do you know me?"

I paused and regarded him again. Then I admitted, "No, sir, I do not recognize you."

He laughed, a gamin-like cackle for a man who had seemed rather reserved. "I'm Jack Wiggins."

"And what brings you here, Jack Wiggins?" The name meant nothing to me.

"I have been looking for someone all day. Fate seemed to bring me to Baker Street and then I glanced up at 221B and saw you, sir, in the window. No wonder you don't know me, governor." He suddenly spoke in a Cockney accent. "I was a lad of twelve when last I stood in this room."

"My word. Did we have any child clients? I really don't remember."

"Not a client, Dr. Watson." He resumed his refined tone. "An ally. I was kept in the employ of Mr. Holmes."

"By Jove, one of the Irregulars," I said, offering to shake hands with him again.

"The leader. I reported directly to Mr. Holmes. You remember the river chase and the Agra treasure?"

"Ah, yes. I wrote it all up as 'The Sign of the Four.' That's a case I shall never forget. In pursuing that treasure, I came into contact with a real treasure, Miss Morstan. God rest her soul. My sweet second wife."

"Really, sir," he responded respectfully.

"And what has life dealt to you?" I asked. I could see

that he had quite risen above his origins as a street urchin. I offered him a glass of port.

"Can you guess, Dr. Watson?" He smiled openly at me.

"No," I said. "Holmes could, but I can only see that you have the look of an honest man, and a kind one, if I don't miss my guess. And one who has risen by his own efforts in this world."

"Thank you, sir. That last is not exactly right, though. It was Mr. Holmes who helped me rise."

"Really?" I had never known Holmes to go in for any sort of philanthropy.

"Yes. And I should never have known it *was* Mr. Holmes who sent me to school and started me on the way up if I had not used some of Mr. Holmes's own methods to find out."

"I'm quite enchanted." I pulled the pipe from my mouth and said, "Holmes has been dead now for two years. Only yesterday, I set about to write his biography. What has life and Holmes made of you, my boy? It would be a fascinating chapter for the biography."

"Sherlock Holmes was a great influence upon me," he began. "And, so, sir, were you."

"I?" I leaned forward with keen interest.

"Holmes used to point you out to me and say, 'There is a good man and a steady one. Consider his profession, my young friend.'"

"You have become a physician?"

"Yes. But of a special sort, you know. A consultant. I am a consulting psychiatrist at St. Giles Hospital."

"Consulting?"

"Like Mr. Holmes with Scotland Yard, I am not on the

regular staff. I am brought the special cases. Those whose maladies, whose inner secrets, whose perversions, whose repressed desires have baffled the probing of my colleagues."

"Let me congratulate you on having undertaken so exacting and fatiguing a career."

"That it is, my dear Dr. Watson. One that often holds nasty surprises and grievous setbacks."

"All physicians have their failures," I reminded him gently. "Even the great consulting detective had a few failures."

I could have reminded him of one of Holmes's failures: Irene Adler, whom I had just remembered the night before, though she had lain dormant in memory for many decades. With what scorn Holmes used to say "the woman," meaning she who had escaped his snare and made her way to the Continent so many years ago. I wrote it up in "A Scandal in Bohemia."

Wiggins spoke again, "All day and into the night I have been in pursuit of a patient who escaped."

"Escaped!" I said. "How extraordinary."

"She is an extraordinary patient. I've scarcely ever known anyone so intelligent. She has a marvelous facility with locks. Throughout her years of incarceration, she has simply let herself out. At will."

"But she returns?"

"Yes. In the past she has returned as she went. When she pleased." Wiggins stretched his feet toward the fire. "She is much older now and the cold being vicious, I felt I needed to find her. I must concede: she has eluded me."

My mind returned to the biography. "Do you have any of Holmes's old letters?"

"Holmes wrote to me from time to time. I have preserved all of his letters."

"And might I see them? For the biography?"

Wiggins was silent. I could read his thoughts. He hesitated to unveil this heretofore unknown facet of Holmes's character.

"Dr. Watson, I would like to be of assistance to you, but this is a matter that requires some thought." Wiggins was looking around the room. His glance travelled up and down my figure as though he were assessing my situation. "Would you come around tomorrow to St. Giles and speak with me there?"

"Certainly."

"You may be interested in some of the patients, and in my dog, Toby. He joins me in my work."

"Toby? The tracking hound?"

Wiggins laughed. "Not like the Toby you once had. This Toby is not a nose. My Toby helps me to relate to the patients; he's a companion dog. Patients will respond to a friendly animal sometimes even though they cannot communicate with people."

"Wiggins," I ejaculated, "I saw an old woman with a dog companion just outside, just before you arrived."

"A mongrel with a white plume-like tail?"

"The same!"

"Which way did they go?"

"North, up Baker Street around the corner to the left."

Wiggins grabbed his coat and ran from the apartment exclaiming, "Ten o'clock, tomorrow, St. Giles," as he went.

And though he took his leave, my lonely chambers felt less lonely because an old acquaintance had visited. I stood at the window and watched his dark form disappear up the street. The bowler so like my own was clamped again to his head, his step lively and determined.

There is a good man and a steady one, Holmes had told the lad of me. Holmes had set me up as an example to a bright but footloose urchin. And the boy had turned out all right. Yes, that was clear enough, even if the snobs wouldn't have him on the regular staff.

I poured myself a snifter of brandy and took my familiar seat beside the fire, and the wind roared and howled like a child in the chimney.

Before long it was time to go to bed, and I took my candle and went once more into Holmes's old chamber. Again I felt the dankness of the icy linen when first I crawled into bed. I studied the pattern on the wallpaper, dark floral arabesques, and, in my drowsy state, those patterns began to swirl like fog, taking first one shape and then another. All the shapes were of Holmes and myself in our youth. I saw us as though we were sitting on a train, facing each other, going out to the countryside where Holmes was needed, and the wind-blown landscape streamed past our faces. I could hear the clacking of the great steel wheels as they rushed over the tracks.

At one point I seemed to hear rustling from my own bedchamber, and then movement from the sitting room. I tossed, turned, and listened to the clock striking through midnight.

At one o'clock I thought I heard the soft ding of another bell. I saw a glowing mass of light in the room with me. Half-asleep, half-awake, I thought the apparition of the Christmas tree had come to haunt me again. But this was an oval of light, shaped like the frame for a portrait. The glow was gentle at first, but it increased in intensity until it was all aglitter and hurt my eyes to look. It hovered in the air above the carpet, where it shimmered and sparkled.

Then a voice emanated. from the light. It was the familiar voice of my old friend, but stern: "Look again, Watson. Look at the books again."

When I entered the sitting room, the front door was ajar! Cold air from the hall streamed in. My next clear memory was of myself standing before the sideboard. I held my candle above the books. A new volume had been placed on the sideboard! Opened to V! Someone had been looking at the V volume in the commonplace set of books. *Violin?* Why, the entry was razored out! V, Violin!

My head whirling, I seated myself in the visitor's chair. This was recent work. I had not left the V volume on the sideboard. Frantically, I thought of the buff-coloured note and its warning. I had been too hasty in dismissing it.

What could I do but secure my lodgings? I pushed a chair against the door to the hall and then another chair. Back in Holmes's bedroom, I moved a heavy washstand athwart that door.

The apparition I had seen in the window wielded a musical instrument. For a moment I seemed to stand again in the street below, to look up to the three arched windows, to see the silhouette of Holmes and the familiar gesture of lifting the violin to his chin. But wearing his cap and coat. A figment of fancy.

But someone *had* definitely been in the apartment, despite the locked door—someone with a razor. Had the apparition of Holmes not awakened me, would I have become the intruder's helpless victim?

❧ 3 ❧

BLOOD

WHEN I PRESENTED myself to the doorkeeper at St. Giles, my Royal College of Physicians' card and my mention of Dr. Wiggins quickly gained my admittance to the famed mental hospital. Rays of the winter sun fell through a domed skylight that had been set with a few triangles of coloured glass. Pretty blotches of light scattered here and there on the sunlit floor. As is always the case with such a place, it seemed sanitary without being truly clean. None of the brightness which is the hallmark of private cleanliness sparkled here. And I suppose I may as well record that even in this anteroom there was something of an odour, reminiscent of my old days as an intern at St. Christopher's. Ammonia—stale urine. Not a pleasant perfume, but almost impossible to mask or eradicate in these public hospitals.

The lobby was quiet, and I heard the toenails of a dog clicking on the marble floor. Instantly, the very mongrel that I had seen out my window appeared, with Dr. Wiggins at his heel. In his starched coat, he looked like the wisest and most able man in London.

"Your dog has returned, I see." I stroked the beast's head. He was an exceptionally pleasant animal, looking into my eyes with something like affection.

"And the patient returned as well." He put his arm through mine. "Perhaps, I could show you a bit of the hospital before we talk."

We proceeded to the interior of the hospital, halting at a cross-corridor when a great troupe of men, who Wiggins said had been to chapel, filed past us. It was indeed a sad sight to see so many men, so various, suffering from mental illnesses, proceeding with strange limping or crab-like gaits. Some of the men scowled to see me and the doctor, and one vigorous fellow waved both of his hands in my face. I looked in scores of pairs of eyes, and there it seemed I saw suffering on suffering. Often the skin of their faces looked red or peeled or sallow, and their hair, while not unkempt, seemed to have been combed by a distracted hand.

Then another door opened and out poured a similar band of women, an even more distressing sight for one who has ever been an admirer of women. Their eyes were pitiful, often of the saddest blue. Some of them had mask-like faces. Others walked with their eyes closed, while mumbling incoherently. Their number seemed equal to that of the men, but the sound of their feet, their heels coming down, was variegated, like the patter of rain falling on different objects.

Suddenly, out of the crowd, an old woman darted toward me. She looked nimble and strong. She positioned herself squarely in front of me. Wiggins's hand tightened on my arm. Her eyes glared madly into mine, and she spoke: "You have been in Afghanistan, I perceive?"

At this pronouncement, I fainted dead away.

I opened my eyes to see both their faces bent over me. The lined, old face of the woman came in and out of focus, but each time her eyes appeared mad and strangely intelligent.

"Madame," I said, "who are you?"

"Nannerl," she said. She stood up and backed away. "Nannerl," she said again over her shoulder. A name like a snarl.

At this point, attendants escorted her away, and Wiggins helped me to my feet. "Let's get to an office," he said. With Wiggins steadying me, we passed through the corridor. The patients regarded me with new curiosity, as though I might be one of them.

"Who is she? I believe she hates me."

"Nannerl is the patient who escaped last night."

When we reached the office Wiggins used for consulting, he had me sit in a big Morris chair. From a drawer in the desk, he produced a bottle of sherry and poured me a generous portion.

"She was in the street outside my apartment with the dog."

"Yes, I think she was. Now tell me, John," he said, "what was it in the woman's greeting that so upset you?"

"I see you have not read my works."

"Come, don't be petulant." He leaned across the desk and put his hand on a leather-bound volume, stamped in gold. "I have your works preserved in style. I *have* been re-reading. Just explain like a good chap. Her greeting?"

"She's a very clever person, your patient. She quoted Holmes's initial observation of me. We had only been introduced by young Stamford when Holmes observed that I was returned from service in Afghanistan. This he deduced from merely looking at me. But she could not have made the same deduction. I have not been in Afghanistan for decades. She wished to upset me, and she succeeded admirably in doing so."

Wiggins sat quietly, but his eyes began to sparkle. "And what would be the value in upsetting you?" he finally asked, but it was a question I could not answer.

Then he went to a cabinet and removed a file folder. Its tab read *Family Name Unknown—Patient A.*

"Here are some Christian names that our patient has used over the years. Only first names—Dorothy, Fanny, Augusta, Nannerl. We have so little background on her," he went on. "There was a fire in the document room soon after she was admitted. Only a very few records were destroyed, but hers was among them. Tomorrow she may give you another name, or she may go on for years with the same name."

"The diagnosis?"

"Here is a list of doctors who have seen her over the years and their diagnoses—amnesia, hysteria, paranoia, finally schizophrenia."

"Which is *your* diagnosis?"

"Mine reads: 'Mental illness of unknown etiology. Cannot be accurately diagnosed.' She seems to be a resident more than anything else. General intelligence is high. Tradition has it that Nannerl signed herself in over thirty years ago—a volunteer to the care of St. Giles."

Looking up from the records, Wiggins added, "She dislikes Toby, though he is devoted to her. Complains of his bark. Almost G-sharp, but off-key, I've heard her say."

"The dog was concerned about her last night," I commented.

"She has been exceptionally agitated and confused for two days."

A sister suddenly appeared holding out a buff-coloured note. "Sir," she said, "this just came for you. Left by an old woman dressed all in red."

As soon as the sister left us, Wiggins opened the note and began to read. First he looked very sober, then he began to laugh.

"Look at this, John," he said, "but brace yourself." He handed me the buff card; the handwriting and ink were familiar. It read,

> *Dear Dr. Wiggins,*
>   *Do not contribute to the biography of Sher-*
> *lock Holmes. Discourage its being written at all.*
>   *Mrs. John H. Watson*

"An outrage!" I said. Who was this presumptuous woman in red? "You know Mrs. Watson is deceased. What does this mean?"

"I don't know."

"I received a warning note written on the same stationery, written by the same hand. These communications seemed to be precipitated by my advertised intention to write a definitive biography of Holmes."

"Some old enemy, perhaps?" Wiggins mused.

"Possibly," I said. "Let me question Nannerl. The two women may be connected."

Dr. Wiggins began to pace back and forth in his office. Finally he said, "Forgive me, John. I cannot permit that. You are upset. She will become upset in response. This is not the time for you to conduct research."

"What have you decided about the letters Holmes sent to you?" I regret that I spoke with some irritation and impatience.

Wiggins answered slowly, "I feel that I must protect the privacy of my benefactor."

"You have been swayed by this note!"

"Not at all. My mind was quite made up."

Disappointment engulfed me like mist. I paused, trying to think of the next step. Finally, I asked, "Will you at least let me see Nannerl another day?"

Though Wiggins hesitated, he reluctantly agreed.

"Tomorrow," I insisted, rising to leave. "May I come back tomorrow?"

"Very well," he consented. "Since you wish it so much."

When he turned the knob to open the office door for me, something acted as a doorstop. Wiggins leaned his shoulder to the panels, and the door swept a fan of blood over the floor. Behind the door lay the inert body of the dog Toby, whose throat had been cut. The incision was long and neat.

Wiggins knelt, stricken with grief. He stroked the dog's head tenderly, saying, "Toby, oh, Toby."

The dog's features were twisted in a grotesque grimace. Gently, Wiggins slid the limp carcass inside his office. "Why?" he said to me.

We could only gaze at each other. I thought of Nannerl, but did not speak. Just an hour before, the little hound had been full of life and willing obedience.

"Come." Wiggins took my arm. "Let me see you to the front door."

As he ushered me out of his office, we were both obliged to step over the smear of blood.

Though the cab carried me through streets lined with tinsel and holly, my mood was far from festive. Would Nannerl, a frail old woman, be so cruel as to slaughter an innocent animal? Was the same razor used to remove pages from my records?

Why did the woman in red use my own name so familiarly?—*Mrs. John H. Watson*, indeed!

4

ASSAULT

Soon after I arrived home at 221b Baker Street, I received an invitation from Wiggins. He asked me to attend a performance of *Messiah* at St. Paul's as his fiancée, a Miss Lucinda, was singing. I was pleased that even though he would not assist me with the biography, nonetheless, he wished to have cordial relations.

When night came, another thick fog came with it, and the carriage parted veils of grey as Wiggins and I rolled toward St. Paul's. Endeavouring to be entertaining, I explained to my host that the sixty-foot columns within St. Paul's did not support the dome, though they appeared to do so.

"Sherlock Holmes, disguised as a worker, discovered that the columns are actually free-standing. They miss the ceiling by one inch."

I hastened to explain that this was all in accordance with Sir Christopher Wren's design. When the building committee had insisted on supporting columns, Wren had been forced to appear to give in to them. Holmes had studied a copy of the original plans, and he had correctly deduced that Wren was too proud an architect to succumb to the cautious committee. When workmen were recruited to clean the ceiling, Holmes got himself on as a labourer.

When I finished speaking, Wiggins pointed out the carriage window at the indistinct shapes passing in the fog.

"It's as though they're all shades," Wiggins murmured.

At last the massive cathedral appeared. Mellow light spilled from the doors, and the lights of many carriages and autos surrounded and wreathed the great church. By twos and threes, sometimes in parties of eight or ten, a great mass of people was being funneled into St. Paul's. I felt pleased to walk among the throng and to be a participant in the Christmas celebration.

"Dr. Watson!" a stern voice boomed out of the fog.

I turned to see the bulk of Mycroft, Sherlock's brother!

"A word with you." Mycroft was old but gigantic. His face sagged like the tallow of a warm candle. "You have been so ill-advised, sir," he began without further pleas-antries, "as to announce your intention of writing my brother's biography. I forbid it." And with that he turned abruptly, strode rapidly away, and disappeared into the church.

I was stunned to see Mycroft. I considered pursuing him, setting up an appointment for an interview. But I knew in my heart that Mycroft would be as silent and unmovable as a boulder.

"You see, my dear Dr. Watson," Wiggins murmured, "I am not alone in wishing to leave Holmes's missing pages unwritten."

We were early enough to find seats near the altar and to have time to chat and to look about at the blazing candles and the greenery. Wiggins claimed that Lucinda was an extraordinary singer and often performed for charitable purposes.

I think that I have never enjoyed *Messiah* or any music so much. It was performed properly in the astringent baroque style; the silvery high trumpet was both martial and ethereal.

When Lucinda began to sing, Wiggins suddenly leaned forward. She *was* a singer of particularly wonderful voice, but with hollow cheeks and, I thought, rather too thin. She sang with great pathos a contralto solo—"He Shall Feed His Flock."

At the sound of her lovely voice Wiggins's face took on a glow that I had not seen there before. I half-remembered that once I had seen Holmes transported like that while listening to music. Violin music, I believed. Sigerson! Yes, it was Victor Sigerson whose playing had all but bewitched Holmes. Long ago.

Wiggins's knuckles were white—he was gripping the armrest with such force. Lucinda had marvelous volumes of breath on which to float her melody. I thought all the audience was moved by her song of the Nurturing Shepherd.

Someone else was also terribly moved by the song. An old woman, stylishly and brightly dressed in cerise, began to weep. What had the sister said? *An old woman, dressed in red.* Was this the woman who had left the note identifying herself as *Mrs. John H. Watson?*

I nudged Wiggins and nodded in her direction. Her

head turned and, despite the crowd, she caught our eye. At once, she jumped to her feet and hurried from her pew.

Like Holmes, Wiggins exclaimed, "Watson, the game's afoot." Simultaneously, we rose from our seats and moved to the exit. In the street outside St. Paul's there was no sign of her.

Wiggins and I each started off in different directions into the fog. I fancied I could hear her footsteps ahead of me. Sure enough, when she entered the net of light from a streetlamp, I could see her little figure, like a bright bird, scurrying rapidly away.

"Up ahead," I called out, hoping that Wiggins was within earshot and could head her off. But she was gone again in the fog.

There were other pedestrians of the night, and as I charged through the fog their dark forms indistinctly emerged and then retreated into grey mist. Their vague aspects frightened and chilled me. Street lamps, post boxes, people—emerged like obstacles in a dark channel that the boat of my body must avoid.

Suddenly one of the forms—the hunch of its shoulders, its stature and stance—seemed familiar to me. I drew in my breath, for, once again, I felt that I was seeing Sherlock Holmes.

"Holmes!" I cried, but with a catch in my throat.

The head turned. He was startled to hear me call him.

He raised his cane and lunged. "Forget me!" I saw, at the same instant, a blur of red hurl itself from the mist in an attempt to restrain the raised cane. Too late. The shaft of the cane glanced off my brow, and I fell to the pavement.

When I awoke, the face of Dr. Wiggins came into focus. He was bending over me and cradling the back of my head in his hand.

"Holmes, the ghost of Holmes," I mumbled. "But not Holmes." The figure seemed poised over me again, and I shrank back against Wiggins's hand.

"Steady, man," Wiggins said, "Too many shocks in one day."

"Not a silhouette this time, not a violin, but a cane." In memory I envisioned the Holmes of old with his cane raised, ready to annihilate the viper. "'The Speckled Band,'" I whispered.

Wiggins summoned a cab and before long, my head splitting, we were jostling toward Wiggins's lodgings.

In the cozy light of his sitting room, he pronounced my injury not serious and put me to bed on his sofa. My sleep was fitful. Strains from *Messiah*—"Every valley shall be exalted"—besieged me. Again and again I approached arched windows through the night. "Why do the nations so furiously rage together?" Each time the shadow of Holmes appeared, he raised the violin ready to play; sounds like the squeaking of a mouse filled my ear. "Hallelujah! Hallelujah!" an entire chorus roared, brandishing canes above my head.

In the morning, over raspberry compote and a cup of Earl Grey, I told Wiggins of my desire to check the commonplace books for clues pertaining to Nannerl's relationship to Sherlock Holmes. Wiggins proposed that he accompany me to Baker Street. As our carriage passed by

Christmas shoppers, I noticed snowflakes twinkling in the air.

When we arrived, Mrs. Hudson and Mary were in an uproar.

"It was an old man, sir," Mary said. "He had got in your room. He was trying to steal your books."

"An old man with a sharp nose, gaunt cheeks, wearing a plaid overcoat?" Wiggins asked.

"Yes, sir."

"Was this person stealing the books with handwriting in them? The commonplace books?" I asked.

"Why, yes, sir," Mary answered. "I stopped him at the front door."

"Why weren't you here," Mrs. Hudson asked me, "if you two knew what was going on?"

"Now, now," I said soothingly. "How brave Mary was to avert the theft. You see, no harm is really done."

"He had a cruel eye, sir," Mary interjected. "I thought he might strike me. He raised his cane at me."

I exchanged a glance with Wiggins.

Mrs. Hudson put her arm around Mary. "Come, my dear, come and lie down. Everything is all right. Dr. Watson is here now."

Wiggins and I gathered the books and lugged them upstairs to my chambers.

"I should like to read these records alone," I said slowly.

Wiggins said, "I'd like to know why someone wishes, desperately, to keep Holmes's life from being reopened."

"So would I," I said.

"Toby is dead, Mary threatened, and you, yourself, attacked." His solicitude pleased me. He went on, "I can't in easy conscience leave you. Suppose you were to nod off while you read?"

"Oh, I doubt that I'll sleep over this. But I'll barricade the door. Anyone could silently pick a lock, but to get past a furniture barricade would cause a noisy scraping."

After Wiggins left, I immediately turned my attention to one of my own early notebooks in the stack. Apparently I myself would add pieces to the puzzle. In any case, I would need to re-read all of this material for the biography.

The N from Holmes's commonplace books was at hand. Nannerl of St. Giles had known Holmes's exact greeting to me. Had Holmes known her? I turned the pages toward *Nannerl*—but there was no such entry. There was NANCE and then, at the bottom of the left-hand page, an entry began NEUSCHWANSTEIN. And then! The pages on the right-hand side, like the V pages, had been razored out! Whatever Holmes had had to say about it NEUSCHWANSTEIN had disappeared. "Bavarian castle, built by Ludwig II . . ." the notation began.

I paced around the room trying to steady my nerves and to dissipate my vexation. I stopped at the window. The bright mica-like flakes of snow had changed to great wet blobs. They seemed to be pouring from the sky, and already snow was piling up against the kerb and against the lamp posts.

I dusted off my own old marbled notebook. It was an apprentice writer's notebook. Here I had experimented with writing in the present tense. I had begun to practice compositions—observations—before attempting my successful chronicles of Holmes's career as a consulting detective. Holmes and I were but newly acquainted. I opened the notebook, and then a stroke of luck came to my assistance. Some of these pages were only *half-torn*.

Yes. Someone had begun to tear away the relevant pages, but then, fearing detection, had attempted to carry off the books themselves. These were the very pages from the past that he had wished me not to read! Irrelevant though they might seem, in them was the end of the thread that would eventually lead me through the maze.

Although I read of the past, it bloomed before me as though it were the present.

II

THE
PAST

❧ I ❧

SHERLOCK HOLMES
INSPECTS A VIOLIN

MR. SHERLOCK HOLMES is sitting with me here, in the year of Our Lord, 1886, at our lodgings on Baker Street. He is at times a most inconsiderate fellow-lodger, having but lately filled the entire apartment with the malodourous by-product of a chemical experiment that he assures me is necessary in solving some mystery. Fortunately it is a fine spring day, and I have just opened the windows. But what will it be like to be cooped up with this fellow during the winter?

"You wish to know what I was burning just now?" Holmes asks me.

"Not at all," I assure him. If this sharing of rooms is to continue, I judge it necessary to take no undue interest in his work, and I hope that he will not exhibit too much curiosity about mine.

"Then why, when you went to open the window, did you take the most circuitous route, past the deal table, and why did you pretend to drop your little notebook so that you could linger and get a better look into the beaker?"

Did not such a mischievous expression lurk around his eyes as he spoke, I would be unspeakably offended by his exaggeration of my actions.

"Well observed!" I say heartily.

"And correctly observed," he insists. "I am burning a bit of varnish scrubbed from the side of a certain fiddle that is purported to be of some antiquity."

"And why might you be doing that?" I inquire.

Holmes saunters to the window and then calls me to come and look out. As I approach I hear the sound of what I take at first to be a most marvelous bird. The notes tumble merrily through the open window. Then I recognize that these warblings are developing into a tune. I stand beside Holmes, who is looking out with satisfaction.

"'The Bird-Catcher's Song,'" he says, "from Mozart's *The Magic Flute*." Holmes stretches himself, and he stretches his long neck from his shirt collar as though *he* were some exotic bird, an ostrich perhaps. "And rather accurately whistled," he says. "Now what do you suppose is the profession of that gentleman who is coming to see us and whose inquiries will shortly return us to the subject of varnish?"

"A keeper at the aviary," I suggest.

"Not at all," Holmes speaks with some disdain. "Notice how his head is carried on one side."

Indeed, it looks as though the man below on the street might have observed, for too long, the cocked head of a parrot. But I hold my peace. Mr. Sherlock Holmes is rather fond of forcing me to draw conclusions about this or that and then mocking me if I'm wrong.

"Of course he is a flautist. And he is whistling a part that will be performed tonight. In last night's paper you will find a review by Mr. Bernard Shaw, the music critic, quite extravagantly complimenting the execution of this tune. But here comes the rascal."

"And why do you call him a rascal?" I ask.

"Because he is a liar," says Mr. Holmes. "He has engaged my services, but he does not tell me the whole truth."

I hear a rhythmic knocking at our front door, and a pause just long enough for the flautist to tell Mrs. Hudson, our landlady, that he wishes to call on my fellow-lodger. Then immediately the shrill and exuberant whistling resumes as he walks up our stairs.

"You hear," says Sherlock Holmes, "how he is rather overdoing it. He wishes to appear nonchalant and self-confident."

In fact, the tune is now at a piercing and unpleasant volume. When Mr. Holmes opens the door, this young dandy leans for a moment against the door jamb and finishes whistling the phrase before speaking. He takes off his top hat and attempts to whirl it on the end of his finger, but it goes flying away and lands on the sideboard over a plate of uneaten toast.

"Dear, dear," says Holmes, "come in," and he retrieves the top hat. He himself twirls it up in the air, catches it, and sends it twirling again across to our visitor. In fact, it lands on his head.

"Good," the whistler says, with a decided German accent.

Holmes introduces me to the fellow: Hans Bachaus. I

notice that Mr. Holmes's lip is curling a bit. Mr. Bachaus is beautifully dressed with a lavender scarf at his throat and a bit of spring lilac in his buttonhole. The lilac odour beckons me powerfully, and I determine to leave Holmes alone with his guest and to avail myself of the springtime by taking a stroll in Hyde Park. I make overtures to do so, but Holmes insists that I stay.

"I'll walk with you in a few moments," he says, "if you will but wait while I give my report to Mr. Bachaus here."

Actually it is my preference to go alone, having had the desire to absent myself from Holmes's company for a while, but Holmes is so polite about his request that I cannot refuse.

"May I congratulate you," Holmes continues, "on the excellent notice the orchestra received for its performance last night. Had the singers only been the equal of the instrumentalists doubtless Mr. Shaw would not have written that your group would be better suited for the Scottish Highlands than for London."

"It is not my fault," the flautist says with no concern. "My performance was 'impeccable.' 'Transporting.'" he adds, performing a little pirouette, much to my amazement. "And what about the violin, Herr Holmes? Shall I advise my friend that it is an authentic Guarnerius, that he should purchase it—no delay?"

"Of what calibre performer is your friend?" Holmes asks.

"He is almost my equal," says the German dandy, inspecting his fingernails and burnishing them on his sleeve.

"And is he your equal in lying?" Holmes asks pleasantly.

"Ach!" screeches the flautist. "If you wish to be insulting, I will leave."

"As you wish," Holmes says calmly. "I will send my results to the Munich Opera Orchestra, to Hans Bachaus. Of course that worthy gentleman will be puzzled since he has never set foot in these rooms. I wonder if he will be able to deduce that you, the third-chair flautist, Mr. Karl Klaus, have borrowed his name and would like to borrow his glory while in London."

The lower lip of the flautist begins to tremble.

"You have discovered my secret," he says stammering. Not at all the cocky young jay he pretended to be.

"But I have not discovered the necessity for your lie," says Holmes. "I would as soon test the varnish for you as for the real Mr. Bachaus."

"It was not my fault," Klaus says. "My friend, who insisted that you alone were to conduct the test, also insisted that I assume another name. I thought there was no harm in taking that of Bachaus. I do play the flute. How did you know?"

"Both yesterday when you first came and today you made an error in whistling."

"Impossible!" regaining some of his arrogant pretentiousness.

"Not in intonation. Your sense of absolute pitch has not played you false. But in rhythm. It is slightly inexact. The end of the phrase is held too long. Bachaus would never make the error. At least not without Mr. Shaw's having remarked on it. It is just the sort of mistake that would have drawn Shaw's ridicule. He did not ridicule; therefore, the error did not occur in the performance. You always make the error; therefore, you are not Bachaus."

"But how did you know my true name?"

"You told me. It is written on the band of your hat, which you were so kind as to toss onto the toast."

"Remarkable," I cannot help but put in. "What a quick eye you have, Holmes."

"Elementary, my dear Watson. And what is your friend's name?"

"Sigerson," replies the humbled Karl Klaus. "Please question me no further. On my oath, I say nothing about Victor."

I judge Klaus to be firm in this resolve, and so apparently does Holmes, for he does not pursue the line of questioning. "No, it is not authentic. The violin is not a Guarnerius."

"Too bad," Klaus says. "Victor was very fond of it."

"Perhaps he should buy it anyway," puts in Holmes, "if he likes the tone. 'What's in a name?'"

"He likes to know the origins of things. This will put him off," Klaus says.

"Well, I have wasted quite enough time with you," Holmes says. "My friend here is waiting impatiently for his walk in Hyde Park. As for you, Karl Klaus, take your miserable self from these premises. Consult me no more on any matter. No, I will not accept your money. Very simply, I wish never to see you again. Kindly do not whistle under my window."

Holmes is a bit pompous in all this, but the fraudulent dealer in violins is ready to leave under any conditions. No sooner has he gotten away, then Holmes doubles up in silent laughter.

"There is a young man of such consummate stupidity that I am sure, Watson, you can predict exactly what my next move will be."

I am quite amazed by this.

"Has he gotten around the corner yet?" Holmes asks.

I stick my head out into the balmy air and see the long scissor-like legs of the dandy take him out of sight.

"Quick, Watson," says Holmes. "Far from never wishing to see that young rascal again, I am most curious about him. We'll follow him and learn more about this Sigerson and the other members of the Munich Opera Orchestra."

So out we go—*not* in the direction of Hyde Park, as Holmes has led Klaus to believe, but hot on Klaus's footsteps. It is a relief to be outside. The sun is shining warmly. There on the street corner is a wagon loaded with fresh flowers from the country. Daffodils fill the cannisters of cold water, and the pungent aroma of hyacinth and lilac is everywhere. The spring is early, and I notice that many shop doors are propped ajar and that windows of the upper floors are open. Occasionally we hear people happily exclaim about the sunshine and warmth.

"Why are you bothering with this?" I ask Holmes. "He is no longer your client, and you wouldn't even accept the fee that was rightfully yours."

"For its own sake," Holmes answers gaily. "It's spring, and the spring air has whetted my appetite to know, to understand any little concealment that may come before me."

Alas, when most young men experience a heightened interest in sociability, in going to dances and eating on the grass as the season warms, all that this Holmes wants to do is to solve silly and inconsequential mysteries. He is walking briskly, and evidently he is in an excellent frame of mind.

"Besides," he goes on, "if Sigerson refuses to buy this violin, the varnish of which I have just now analyzed with care, then I may wish to make an offer myself."

"Really, Holmes, you already have a fiddle."

"Yes, but I do not own a Stradivarius."

"A Stradivarius?"

Holmes laughs out loud with delight and actually fairly leaps from the kerb into Portland Place. "Yes," he says gleefully. "So perturbed was our former client in being discovered in his little business of lying that he failed to ask me what I had discovered from an examination of the ash of the varnish and from its chemical analysis."

Now I begin to understand why Holmes did not wish to accept any fee from the client. He is rather scrupulous.

"I would have told him," he goes on, "if he had asked me. But you observed, did you not, that his only question was whether the violin was a Guarnerius. I told him the truth: it is not. And had he asked, I would have told him the further truth: what it *is*."

"Naturally, he had no idea that you possessed the power to do so," I say. Holmes's air of superiority can be irritating.

"It is not my fault, as *he* likes to say, if he vastly underestimated my powers." The door is open to a pastry shop and layers of aromas sweep over us.

"And why did he want you to analyze the varnish?"

"He was unsure of what he had in his possession. How would he have responded if I had said, 'Amati'?" Holmes queries.

"The German would have jigged for joy."

"And what would he have said if I had said, 'Stradivarius'?"

"That is scarcely believable. Are you sure, Holmes?"

We walk on down Regent till our German stops beyond Piccadilly Circus to admire a window full of light spring gloves. We hesitate accordingly in front of a haberdashery.

Holmes tents his hands in satisfaction. "Chemistry does not mislead us," he says. He shoots me his shrewdest glance. "What science has told us, a royal ear—the ear of an artist capable of making the most discriminating distinctions concerning the timbre of sound—has told the man considering purchasing the violin."

"Really, Holmes!"

"I should like to make the acquaintance of such an ear."

Karl Klaus disappears into a small hotel on Bow Street located across from the Royal Opera House. The windows of the hotel are thrown open. While we are yet half a block away we can hear emanating from an upper window strains of violin music. But they have a most extraordinary effect on Mr. Sherlock Holmes. He *has* been all fine feeling and forward motion. He *has* been giddy with his own powers and gaily following the trail of a very minor criminal. Suddenly his confident gait changes: he begins to walk noiselessly and then up on tip-toe. He indicates to me that I, too, am to walk silently on tip-toe. His features are struck with awe: he walks with one ear thrust forward. His eyes are glazed.

"What is it?" I ask. (My ear for music is rather undeveloped.)

"Hush," he says.

When we reach the hotel, he stops and leans against the brick wall under the open window from whence pours the music. It is rather complicated.

Holmes turns pale.

"Shall we not follow Klaus into the building?" I ask.

Holmes absent-mindedly shakes his head, and it is clear that something of much greater importance to him has replaced the pursuit of Karl Klaus. Only when the tune is over does Holmes mutter, more to himself than to me, "Ravishing."

Then his eyes snap back into focus. "Quick, Watson," he says, "you must go into the building, ask directly for Klaus, tell him that you wish to buy the fiddle, tell him that I am a boor whose behaviour embarrassed you, but above all find out who occupies the room on the front, on the corner of the second floor."

"Really, Holmes, do you feel well? Do you really wish to ask me to perform this errand for you?"

He looks me full in the eye and says with earnest pleading, "I know that I have no right to ask it of you. I have contaminated our suite with chemical smoke; I have redirected the path of your intended walk; I have spoken with insufferable arrogance on a number of topics. But for the sake of the friend that I will become to you, please do me this favour."

Well, one can hardly deny such a heartfelt request, especially from a man like Holmes who is usually dry and ironic in all his conversation.

I enter the hotel—a rather dingy place. It is the sort of place, one of genteel shabbiness, where one would expect to find travelling orchestras of less than first rank. I approach the desk clerk and ask for the room of Mr. Karl Klaus. It, too, is on the second floor, and I begin the climb up. Several gentlemen from the orchestra squeeze around me on the stair. I say squeeze because they carry bulky instrument cases, double basses, trombones, and the like. Most are rather florid-faced Germans of middle age and sporting large handlebar mustaches. As I walk down the corridor on the second floor, I can hear the vibrant violin music resuming. Indeed, the fiddler has the room next to that of Karl Klaus, upon whose door I knock.

When he sees me, he steps back in horror.

"Not blackmail," he protests. "I will not pay. It is not my habit to sell violins under the wrong name. I didn't know."

"My dear sir," I say, "please be assured that my mission has nothing whatsoever to do with blackmail."

"Really?" he says, still not inviting me in.

I remember Holmes's instructions, and I begin as best I can. "You must understand that the opinions of Mr. Holmes have nothing to do with my own point of view." I pause, hoping to be invited in. "To make a short matter of it," I say, "I believe that I would like to purchase the violin myself."

"But why?" Klaus asks, puzzled.

I am forced to stutter for a moment and then say, "It is my way of apologizing for the boorish fellow with whom I live."

"Ach, *mein Herr,* I comprehend," Klaus says. "I didn't get *l'image exactement* with you." He winks at me, and puts a paw on my shoulder. "Come in."

"I can't stay," I say brusquely, and shrug off his hand. I will not allow Holmes to send me into such a situation again. "Tell me what you want for the fiddle, and I'll write you a cheque."

"But don't you wish to play it first?" Klaus asks petulantly.

"I don't perform," I say nervously, "I'm a collector."

"I don't know yet if Sigerson wants it," he says. He is angry at my rebuff.

"And would that be Sigerson next door?" I ask.

"Yes, it is," Klaus responds.

I feel quite relieved to have so easily accomplished a part of the errand on which Holmes has sent me.

"And is that the violin in question which he is now playing?" I add.

"No," Klaus answers. "Is that the sound you wanted to buy?"

"No, no," I assure him. "I don't care about the tone."

"Then what so pleases you about this violin?" he says with a sneer.

"The varnish," I blurt out.

"The varnish?"

"That is, if it is the same colour as the specimen I saw in Holmes's beaker. A lovely colour. A honey colour, a treacle colour."

"Treacle?" he exclaims and laughs rudely. He takes the fiddle out of the case and holds it up. "You like this colour?"

"Ravishing!" I say with as much conviction as possible. "Let me write you a cheque."

"I promised Sigerson first say. *Guten Tag*! I know your

address, and I will send you a note if the violin is on the open market. You may purchase an option to buy now, if you like."

Before I know it, I have written a cheque for £5, and I am descending the stairs without the violin.

Outside, Holmes has changed his location to the portico of the Opera House across the street where he pretends to read a newspaper so that he will be shielded from view. Oddly enough his first concern is not possession of the Stradivarius violin, but the identity of the performer whose music has proceeded unabated.

"Who is it?" Holmes demands eagerly. No offering of thanks for my efforts.

"Sigerson," I reply shortly.

"Sigerson! Then he is undoubtedly already playing the Stradivarius and that accounts for the extraordinary sweetness of his tone."

"Not so," I say. Sometimes the detective is too swift in his deductions.

"Not so?" he says with wonder. "Then what *would* he sound like on the Stradivarius! Watson, I would give my soul to make such a sound."

"Really, Holmes. Isn't this a rather extreme reaction to a fiddler in the Munich Opera Orchestra?"

"The name of his orchestra matters little to me. He will be a concert artist of the first rank. Genius sometimes buds in lowly settings."

I have heard Holmes sawing away on his fiddle, and I really doubt that he is qualified to make such a judgement. Yet the unseen man does perform ably—much better than Holmes. No scraping.

Holmes continues to muse, "Almost, I should let him purchase the fiddle. He deserves to have it far more than I. And yet, his playing is already of the highest order. He scarcely needs any instrument other than the one he now plays."

I begin to describe the outrageous behaviour of Klaus, but Holmes silences me, saying that will keep. He cocks his ear toward the window and while he pretends to read the newspaper, listens with devout attention. Holmes gives me a section of newspaper to read. It is not very interesting. Some suffragettes plan to picket this very Opera House.

Several of the German gentlemen are crossing the street from the hotel and entering the lobby of the Opera House; apparently they are going to rehearse, as none is dressed for performance. Holmes pays them scant attention, but I fear that it will do his scheme for purchasing the violin little good if Klaus sees Holmes and me here, and I try to keep a lookout for him.

Sigerson appears to be winding up his practicing with a few crashing chords in an effect for which I have always judged the violin to be ill-suited. Holmes stares at the window and his eyes glitter with satisfaction.

"Now, Watson," Holmes says, released from the spell and full of energy, "let us step out of the way."

Quickly I explain to him that I, or rather he, cannot purchase the violin unless Sigerson turns it down.

"It is very likely," Holmes says, "that as soon as Sigerson completed the 'Chaconne' Klaus approached him with the question. I will dart into the café and when Klaus comes out, you must accost him. Offer anything you must. I will repay you."

This plan is advanced in the nick of time. Many of the members of the orchestra pass into the hall. I wonder which one is Sigerson, but there are fifteen or twenty men carrying violin cases, and it is impossible to tell. I do stop Klaus, who speaks to me with a curling lip. He quickly tells me that the violin is now sold to Sigerson.

I cannot resist saying, "I suppose that you told him it was not a Guarnerius?"

"I told him the truth—that it was a violin of much value and that the partner of the amateur detective Sherlock Holmes was ready to purchase it at once."

"What makes you think that I'll not tell Sigerson?"

"You assured me as a gentleman that blackmail was not your motive. I assumed that you meant to stay out of an affair that was no concern of yours. Perhaps you, like your friend, are a meddlesome boor?"

I would like to strangle the insolent cur with his own mauve scarf, but instead I turn on my heel and join Holmes in the café.

Now I can see that he is rather keenly disappointed at not obtaining the violin. He scolds himself for failing to make an irresistible offer when he had Klaus at Baker Street. I try to console him by insisting that he accompany me on a real walk in St. James's. When we reach the park, I purchase a nosegay of early roses and lilac and wonder to what young lady of my acquaintance I would most like to present it.

Under the trees, the wheels of prams not used for six months squeak merrily, but this human music has no effect on my friend, nor does the blue sky nor the appearance of little boys' sailboats on the pond catch his eye.

When we return from St. James's to Baker Street, Mrs. Hudson informs us that a note is waiting for Holmes.

"What's this?" he says, brandishing the letter about. "French stationery, German script." He tears the envelope open, and I see that a cheque is enclosed as well as a note.

After reading the note, Holmes seats himself thoughtfully in his chair. He hands me the letter:

> *My dear Mr. Holmes,*
>
> *Please permit me to pay your consulting fee for the varnish analysis. I fear that in one way or another it has not been properly paid. Also, the fact that you attempted to purchase the violin through your agent, Dr. Watson, told me that it was of great value, just as I suspected. Thus you have rendered me a double service.*
>
> *With appreciation,*
Victor Sigerson
>
> *P.S. Do not suppose that our mutual friend Klaus passed on your findings that the violin was not a Guarnerius or that he picked up the hint that it was of great value nonetheless.*

"A very clever fellow, this Victor Sigerson," Holmes muses. "And an artist to boot."

"What insolence," I say angrily. "I really dislike having been made a toady."

"Oh, Watson, you were no more a toady than I," Holmes says cheerfully.

I am surprised to see very little resentment in his

expression. Instead it becomes one of increasingly animated admiration.

"I should like to meet Victor Sigerson," Holmes goes on. "I should very much like to receive a lesson, a violin lesson, at his hands."

"And his taunting letter?"

"There's something playful about his mind." Holmes taps his fingertips together. "I noted it in his performance. Perhaps this letter is really something of a playful challenge."

"What does he think we'll do next?"

"Probably he knows that I will attempt to make his acquaintance. And so I shall."

"Really, Holmes, why bother?"

"Because he is a wonderful artist. He will travel on—perhaps this is the rarest sort of chance to take lessons from someone who will someday be a household word, like Paganini or Tartini. And he has an unusual mind—that will be amusing too. Yes, I will present myself for lessons."

❧ 2 ❧

SNOOKER

HOLMES SITS IN his easy chair by the dead fireplace, presses his long fingers together.

"How do you intend to bring this about?" I inquire.

Holmes paces before the blank fireplace. He goes to the open window and stares onto Baker Street.

"First I think that you and I will have to go on a brief spying expedition. I want to see him in his natural habitat, so to speak."

"What can we possibly find out?" I say. "Why should I be involved at all?"

"It has been obvious to me," says Holmes, "that you have begun to take notes on my activities. I notice, too, that you are making a study of the mysteries of Edgar Allan Poe. You scribble away in your marbled notebook whenever you get the chance. If you want to write something—a lucrative little tale of crime perhaps—that includes the methods of a consulting detective, namely myself, then you must be willing to do the footwork. Just as a concert violinist spends hours practicing, so must you practice your powers of capturing the logic of both the detective and the criminal."

"But there is no crime involved here," I say.

"Yet it is curious that Sigerson, a man of integrity, associates with an impersonator who engages in suspect sales of violins. You must not confine your interest only to the most melodramatic actions."

Holmes is sometimes overly directive. I jump up and fidget with the Persian slipper. It flatters his vanity to think that I may include him in a story. No doubt he hopes that it will send clients his way. Lately few have appeared, I notice.

"Now what we shall do," he goes on enthusiastically, "is to identify Sigerson and then follow him."

Holmes and I sit behind newspapers in the hotel lobby for two hours, until someone addresses a young man as Sigerson. I note that this Sigerson is a tall and aristocratic-looking young gentleman, unlike so many members of the orchestra. He is thin, and he is wearing a soft felt hat with a wide brim, a rather romantic and Werther-like hat. Because of the hat we cannot see much of his face, except he has the arched nose of a hawk. On his nose glitters a pair of square-lensed spectacles with silver rims. He wears a mauve scarf, reminiscent of his friend Klaus.

We follow him and watch him enter a tobacco shop where he purchases a cheroot. Since he would perhaps recognize us if he were to see us (although I am really not sure to what extent he is familiar with our features), we are careful to stay out of sight. He places the cheroot inside his jacket pocket—the jacket is a wine colour and is velveteen, or some other soft and nappy material—and goes back into the street.

Next he enters a tavern, The King's Spur, a smoky den with the portrait of a nude in repose hanging over the bar. A number of rough characters sit drinking mugs of Guinness at the front of the tavern. In the rear of the room, some unsavoury types are gathered around brilliantly lighted snooker tables. Holmes and I slip unnoticed into a booth at the front, as young Sigerson goes promptly to a snooker table.

There he selects a cue from a rack. He chalks the tip, then proceeds to play alone. Carefully, so as not to be noticed, Holmes and I move closer to watch him. It is at once clear that Sigerson is an expert with the cue. Rarely have I seen such easy coordination between the hand and the eye as when he makes his bridge. His hand is illuminated by the bright light hanging over the green felt table. His fingers are thin and delicate. He wears a massive ring of some cheap metal—brass, I would guess. His musician's hands are as perfect for the cue stick as for their work on the delicate violin fingerboard.

Holmes and I have glasses of ale brought to our table, and Holmes hunkers over his glass as much as he can so that he will be inconspicuous. Yet Holmes cannot resist watching Sigerson and throws many a casual and seemingly indifferent glance in that direction.

"Some of the very best musicians have taken an interest in billiards and other table games," Holmes informs me. "Mozart, for example. I think that they find in the movement of the balls, in the use of known laws of impact, some analogue to the structure of music."

Sigerson has a purplish ecchymosis about the size of a thumbprint on the left side of his neck. When I point out this dark patch to Holmes, he tells me that violinists often develop this sort of bruise. Sigerson's firm but delicate jaw line and slender neck would be susceptible to bruising, I should think.

At this moment, Lestrade, a young sergeant from Scotland Yard, enters the establishment. He approaches our table and asks to join us for a pint of bitters.

Holmes quickly tells him that we are in the tavern on business—though he apparently is not—and that we cannot, therefore, ask him to sit with us.

"But if you would do me a favour," Holmes says, "engage that young man in a game of snooker. I should very much like to see how he handles competition."

Lestrade replies, "I don't know that I owe you any favours, but I don't have much to do at the moment. I'll take him on for you if you care to make a wager."

"On whom?" Holmes asks, his eyes sparkling with mischief.

"Well, you must bet on him, of course," Lestrade says.

"Have you watched him practice?" Holmes asks.

"No, I haven't, but have you seen me at work?"

"You mean at play? No, I haven't."

"Then," Lestrade concludes, "we will each be taking something of a chance. I should tell you though that there's not a regular here who would take me on."

"So you work here regularly?" Holmes asks in a rather ironic tone.

"I have to be close to the Opera House. I'm to help with the arrests tonight. You know, of the women."

"The women?" Holmes questions.

"The ones picketing outside the opera. They're stopping the concert audience and annoying people to sign petitions for the suffrage. Next thing you know the dames'll want to sing bass on the stage."

Holmes shrugs. Current events, unless they pertain to crime, are of very little interest to him. With an arrogant swagger Lestrade makes his way to the snooker table.

I explain to Holmes that I've read about the picketing in the morning paper. "They even criticize the plot of the opera as being opposed to the rights of women."

"Mozart had no interest in political causes," Holmes says dryly. "The Queen of the Night is a villain; Mozart was a Mason and believed in the brotherhood of all men. These are good values as far as I'm concerned."

Lestrade's approach to the snooker table does not go unnoticed. Apparently the regulars have all seen him play before, and they gather around. Holmes and I stand up and move closer, carrying our glasses of ale with us.

After the two exchange introductions, we hear Sigerson say, "I prefer to play alone." He looks up at Lestrade with disdain. His expression is cool, almost cruel, and his pronounced jaw is set. "Yet I see you have a following, and so I will give you the pleasure of doing battle with one quite different from yourself."

He speaks English well, much to our surprise.

"After all, Victor is an English name," Holmes says into my ear, "but his dress and manner are quite foreign."

Sigerson's voice is not a very pleasant voice, but there is something confident and self-assured about it. Perhaps a trace of arrogance. Sigerson flexes his nimble fingers in the light, and I notice what a contrast they form with Lestrade's meaty and hairy hands.

The balls are racked and Sigerson breaks, pocketing two red balls. As the game progresses, both players are flawless in their execution, and the murmurs of admirers blend with the click of ivory against ivory. Our thin young man makes a run of several balls and though I never played snooker myself I note his style of playing is unpretentious.

Sigerson concentrates so completely on the game that he takes no notice of spectators. He even ignores his opponent. For him, the entire world seemingly consists only of the rolling balls, green felt, and pockets. The cue seems to be an extension of his arm and hand.

But Lestrade plays to his audience and accepts their congratulations for every success. I can see that he, too, is impressed with the play of Victor Sigerson. Of course in snooker it does not matter how difficult the play is that one sets up so long as one succeeds, but among all good players there is some pressure to make the game as elegant as possible.

Once Lestrade comes close to scratching, but the cue ball jumps out of the pocket.

"Now," Holmes says to me, "this would be the time for Sigerson to make his subtle challenge."

Holmes is right. Sigerson executes the most daring move of the game, a double bank that scores the black ball. The crowd applauds and one chap whistles, but Sigerson refuses to even glance at them.

"He will make an enemy of the crowd," Holmes murmurs, "though he could have them in his pocket, if he chose."

A tall inebriated sailor offers a ten-quid wager on Sigerson. But no one else wishes to bet against Lestrade.

Lestrade sinks a red ball on a long, skillful shot, and he beams at Sigerson with self-satisfaction. As though *that* has put his opponent in his place. But it has not, for once again, Sigerson executes a complex banking maneuver, cueing the ball low to impart reverse English, and scores six points.

This time the crowd openly cheers the frail Sigerson, but he fails to acknowledge their adulation, and one can feel the room turning surly. Someone yells, "Murder the bloke, Lestrade." Taunts and jeers rise from the crowd.

"This will go to Lestrade's head," Holmes says, "but Sigerson would beat him even if there were no spectators at all." Holmes pauses to light his pipe. "Mozart was a formidable player. He composed tunes while he played, too."

As usual, Holmes is quite right, and Lestrade commits the first error of the game, an ill-conceived combination shot that results in a scratch. I suppose that Sigerson will drop back into conservative play to protect his lead now, but I am wrong. Sigerson's next shot is the most spectacular so far! Balls collide with a loud crack and two fly to their pockets at once.

"He has ceased to play Lestrade," Holmes observes quietly. "He is now playing himself. Each play will be more brilliant than the last."

This strategy leads Lestrade to attempt a difficult set-up before he has fully regained his confidence, and his ball comes to rest against the rail, short of the corner pocket. When this occurs, I notice that the crowd all step closer around the players. We both see that the group is trying to intimidate the young man. They begin cracking their knuckles in unison. Holmes and I exchange uneasy glances.

"They shan't injure his hands, Watson!"

Even I am unnerved by the sound of crunching joints.

One man moves so close to Sigerson that when he steps back from having made his play, he bumps the man and is obliged to apologize. This happens again. I wonder that Sigerson does not challenge him! Clearly, Sigerson sees that this bumping is no accident, and he no longer apologizes. Both Holmes and I are outraged that Englishmen would so bully the talented foreigner.

"It's a police tactic," Holmes says grimly. "That's how they control picketers." (While Holmes ignores politics, he knows all the tactics of the police.)

I wonder if many of these men who are Lestrade's friends also work for the Yard. "We can hardly interfere," I say.

"You might try, Watson. After all, you're not going to be applying to him to take you on as a violin student. Just tell him that he has friends here."

I push my way through the crowd. By this time Sigerson is many points ahead of Lestrade, and it is apparent that he is about to win. I shoulder my way through the crowd as though I were going through a bazaar in Afghanistan.

I move closer to Sigerson and stand behind him. He is tall, but slighter of build than he appeared to be at a distance. The crowd is positively hostile in its attitude. I see a little perspiration on his brow, and for the first time he looks around rather anxiously. He stands upright by the edge of the table and tries to survey it nonchalantly. Quickly I say into his ear before he lines up his shot, "You have friends here."

He places his cue stick on the table and swings around and faces me. "Dr. Watson, I presume," he says dryly, "late of the Queen's service."

"Quite right," I say, but as I speak he holds his hand before my mouth and much to my astonishment a red snooker ball appears there!

Immediately the crowd bursts into a loud guffaw— much of it, I fear, aimed at my facial expression of pure amazement.

I have not come forward to be ridiculed for their enjoyment. I shrug my shoulders, but as soon as I make the gesture, he calls attention to it by placing his fingertips atop each shoulder and then revealing two yellow balls. As I retreat back into the crowd—Holmes is suddenly at my elbow—Sigerson begins to juggle.

First the two yellow balls are up in the air, then the red ball he pulled from my lips whirls up and around in the circuit. Now the crowd falls back respectfully.

"Why, he's some sort of magician!" Lestrade exclaims. "No wonder!"

The snooker balls are flying higher and higher into the smoky air, and faster and faster. With an all too graceful movement of the hips, Sigerson breaks open one of his jacket pockets and catches two of them, swivels, and catches the remaining ball in his other pocket.

The room erupts in wild applause.

"What else can you do?" Lestrade asks admiringly.

"What else?" Sigerson says. His voice is faintly mocking though he is careful now not to lose the goodwill that he has bought for himself at my expense. He stares up at the ceiling into the light as though he were transfixed.

"Well, gentlemen," he says, and his voice drops confidentially. "Sometimes I have the gift of reading the past. I can tell you things about yourself that I could not possibly know, except by special telepathic powers."

He pauses and looks around, peering into their faces. They have drawn back from him. He stands alone in the circle of light, and they are like dumb animals held at bay. He has already displayed extraordinary resources, and they are slow to laugh at his preposterous claim.

"Shall I show you?" he asks gravely, very quietly.

Their mood modulates to suit his, and what was a boisterous group becomes quiet and reverential.

"I will need an assistant." The charlatan pauses for dramatic effect. "Someone whom none of you will suspect of having pre-arranged this business for me. Someone to whom I have never spoken before."

They look around at each other. I return to my seat.

"Not one of you. Someone else who is here in the room but who has not stood close to me as I played." He stretches his neck and stands high on tip-toe as he peers toward our table.

"Dr. Watson?" calls Lestrade.

"No, for I have spoken to him—you all saw it," Sigerson objects. "What of the gentleman who is with him?"

"I shall be glad to assist you," says Holmes seriously.

"Please tell everyone present—have I ever spoken to you before?"

"In terms of the strictest meaning of your words—I can assure everyone that you are telling the exact truth."

The listeners seem impressed with Holmes's statement. I see that Holmes is willing to play Sigerson's game, for the words are *only* true in the strictest sense, since Sigerson has indeed communicated with Holmes.

As Holmes begins to walk through the crowd, Sigerson commands, "Come no closer." Then he closes his eyes dramatically. "Without my knowledge I ask you to select objects from several men. Concentrate on one item. You will not hold it up for me to see, but you will become in sympathy with me. Later each object will be returned to its rightful owner. Together we will know things that will astound and confound all those present."

I doubt that *I* shall be confounded by any of Holmes's deductions, but I wonder, can this fellow really receive insights from Holmes? Of course Lestrade knows that this is Holmes the consulting detective, but I think that no one else here knows it; Sigerson has guessed that where I am, Holmes is likely to be also. He has also guessed that Holmes would be willing to assist him in what probably appears to them both to be a very amusing affair.

Sigerson turns his back on the group, and someone blindfolds him. He offers to leave the room entirely, but everyone is content that he can see nothing.

Holmes asks a lad sitting close by if he has a handkerchief. The boy nods—he is a bit frightened—and he produces a crumpled and somewhat stained handkerchief from his hip pocket.

Next Holmes takes a Masonic ring from an elderly gentleman. From several people he takes a letter—whether personal or of a business nature I cannot say at this distance. After the items are collected and placed on Holmes's and my table, Sigerson turns around, flings the bandage from his eyes and says, "First, is it not the case that you yourself are named Mr. Sherlock Holmes?"

"That is correct," replies Holmes. Some in the audience gasp.

"Mr. Holmes, this power has a touch of black magic about it. Do you understand me? Are you willing to participate in black magic as an antecedent to our special powers?"

"Yes," says Holmes, "and I am ready to begin. I shall hold up an object, then I shall point to one of those present. You must tell me if he is the owner."

He holds up the handkerchief and asks if it belongs to the elderly gentleman. Sigerson promptly says that it does not. Then Holmes indicates a member of the Yard. "No," says Sigerson. Then Holmes lays a hand on the black curls of another youth and again Sigerson says, "No." Then Holmes indicates the true owner—"Is it this lad?"—and Sigerson replies, "Yes."

The routine is repeated again and again, each time with perfect success until all the objects have been returned. The crowd is pleased and excited. I wonder what the device is that communicates between them, and how they have been able to arrange it, but none of my hypotheses seems to be verified. Sometimes the object belongs to the second person indicated, sometimes to the tenth—there is no discernable system.

"Now, Herr Sigerson," Holmes says, "you have had your fun, and I have assisted you. For anyone with eyes and ears the matter should be manifestly clear, but since all here see without observing, nothing is clear to them. Do you not agree that your trick is obvious?"

"That it is," says Sigerson, amiably enough.

"But," says Holmes, "even you have observed far less than one could of these people. For example, the lad who owns the handkerchief is without doubt a slab boy. Correct?"

The lad stammers, "That's quite right, sir."

"Further," Holmes continues, "the place of your employment is a recent one. I should judge that you've been there perhaps three days?"

"Exactly," says the boy, looking very uncomfortable.

"Your stool is located close to the west window, and you are new in London."

"Yes," he says, fascinated.

"Your pronunciation and your excellent scarf suggest that you are from the Hebrides Islands."

"And I am," he says beaming. "But how do you know?"

"By observing and not by merely seeing."

Here Sigerson interrupts, "If you deem this an honourable young man, Mr. Holmes, whisper to him a secret of your own and then send him to me. I will tell him what your secret is."

Holmes stands for a moment lost in thought. He is caught off guard by this latest audacity.

"Tell him," Sigerson goes on, "what it is you wish from me. Your request."

At once Holmes bends and whispers in the young printer's ear.

"Gentleman," Sigerson says to the crowd, "do you, too, like Mr. Holmes, believe that this is an honourable chap who will tell the truth?"

The crowd wisely does not commit itself. Certainly I say nothing. This is all a rather cheap show. When the lad reaches the lighted area around the snooker table, Sigerson quickly whispers in his ear.

The lad announces, "That's it. He's right."

Sigerson bows toward Holmes, "And you, sir, shall be given what you wish. Please appear, with Dr. Watson and your instrument, at my room tomorrow morning."

Suddenly, the bright light at the snooker table is extinguished, and the Spur is thrown into gloom. Lestrade immediately strikes a match. All the faces and bodies are as still as figures in a painting. Sigerson has disappeared! As though by magic.

"More than mere legerdemain!" Holmes exclaims.

3

HOLMES BEGINS
VIOLIN LESSONS

THIS SPRING MORNING, in the year of Our Lord, 1886, at our lodging on Baker Street, Mr. Sherlock Holmes is happy as a lark. How extraordinary! That that very self-contained and emotionally undemonstrative gentleman should so let himself go! I have been awakened by the sound of the violin scraping away. Even to my untrained ear the scraping has taken on a new character from the usual melancholy and wandering strains that accompany his thinking as he unravels some hideous or intriguing crime. Now he plays twice as loudly. It is practically a brutal assault. Once he has even turned to me to exclaim (not to ask), "Watson, hasn't my tone a certain richness this morning!"

I do not answer. After a particularly violent assault on three strings at once, he pauses with the bow suspended above the strings and remarks, "How fortunate that Sigerson has especially asked that you be present at my lesson. If you will just bring your notebook along, perhaps you could jot down his points as he makes them. Then long after Sigerson has left London, I will be able to have the continuing benefit of his instruction."

The pleasure of eating breakfast is considerably marred by having to listen to a violin student perform as one eats. I toy with my eggs and grumble, "After all, who is this Sigerson that he should ignite such a fire of enthusiasm in you? Is he Sarasate? No, he is totally unknown."

Holmes tucks the violin under his arm. "You raise more interesting questions than you know, my dear Watson. Yes, you are quite right. He is totally unknown, and who is he?"

"Endlessly fascinating," I say sarcastically.

"I am not being rhetorical," Holmes responds sharply. "I do not think that he is who he says he is, anymore than his pal Klaus was actually Bachaus."

"Really," I say, quite surprised. "Why do you think that misrepresentation is being practiced?" It is a relief to be spared the sound of the fiddle, and I determine to keep Holmes talking until I have finished my breakfast.

"You probably noticed that Sigerson wears a pair of sparkling spectacles?"

"Yes."

"Why does a person who has no visual defect, whose lenses are as ordinary as a well-polished piece of clearest windowpane, why does such a person choose to wear spectacles? Speculate, my dear fellow."

"His glasses are nothing but clear glass! Remarkable. Most people prefer their countenances without the addition of an optical apparatus."

"Perfectly true."

"Perhaps Sigerson wishes to look distinguished or scholarly?" I suggest.

"Exactly. At any rate, he chooses to add a distraction to his face."

"No doubt you noticed his cheap and rather vulgar brass ring."

"Indeed, and the mauve scarf—a distracting colour," Holmes adds.

"And the floppy hat and the poetic velveteen jacket."

"My dear Watson," Holmes says, helping himself to a bite of toast held very daintily so as not to get butter on his fingers, "you have virtually outlined what sounds very much like a disguise."

"But why should he bother with a disguise? We don't care if his name is Sigerson or Schmidt."

"Why indeed?" Holmes turns the screw on his bow in order to tighten the horsehair. "Perhaps during my lesson, you can use the time to glance around his room and to list any items of particular interest that come to your attention. Eh?"

Certainly this proposal makes the morning appear in a slightly more interesting light.

"One thing is not fraudulent about him," Holmes continues, "he is a teacher worth having. His youth is irrelevant. And I would be almost willing to stake my growing reputation as Scotland Yard's last resort that he will someday be a master of considerable renown."

"Unless he becomes a famous snooker player or a stage magician," I add.

Holmes chuckles. "You must understand that he had

worked himself into a tight situation in trouncing Lestrade before his regular admirers. You went to assist him, and assist him you certainly did. Only not quite in the way you had anticipated." Holmes adds rosin to his bow. It is a dry sound that absolutely causes my skin to crawl. "All question about who won the snooker game was entirely dropped."

"Nice of you to forego collecting your bet from Lestrade." I am compelled to cover my ears with my hands and to close my eyes, so much do I dislike the dry rubbing of the horsehair across the round amber cake of rosin.

Holmes taps me on the shoulder with the tip of his bow to signal that he has finished the process. "Not too nice of me," he says. "I shall collect another time."

Holmes and I walk to the Royal Opera House. It is a morning of extraordinary spring beauty, but it is all lost on Holmes, who has no love of nature. Windows are up again today all over London, and the air is soft. The sky is as full of clouds as the bay might be of sailing ships. I buy flowers again from a vendor, though the last ones were presented only to good Mrs. Hudson.

As Holmes and I approach the hotel across from the Opera House, we again hear violin music emanating from the corner room on the second floor. Holmes pauses to listen, checking his memory of the sound, and then he strides forward, apparently satisfied and full of anticipation.

When we enter the room, Sigerson supposes that the flowers are for him. It is really quite quaint. Almost involuntarily he reaches out his hand as though a gift of flowers was to be expected. I inquire about his jaw, which is swaddled in a toothache band.

"Yes, fiendish attack of toothache," he says, "but fortunately on the right side so that it does not interfere with my practicing."

"I should hardly recognize you with that bandage," Holmes says casually. He puts his violin case on the bed and unsnaps the locks.

Sigerson asks Holmes if he would like to try his violin, and Holmes declines, remarking that he is scarcely worthy of a Stradivarius at this point in his development. "Besides," Holmes adds, "I shall probably play better on the violin I am accustomed to. By the way, I have asked Dr. Watson to take a few notes on the remarks that you make."

"I should think that with your unexcelled powers of concentration," Sigerson says, "that any additional notes would be quite superfluous." This is true, and I wonder why I have not questioned Holmes in a similar fashion.

"Nonsense," says Holmes. "All men are fallible; I am a man; therefore, I am fallible."

Sigerson coughs suddenly, but he manages to whip out a gaudy blue and red handkerchief and to cover completely his mouth. I have rarely observed such a startling colour combination. When I blink I seem yet to see those particular shades of blue and red crashing against each other. I make a note of the flamboyant and distracting handkerchief that Sigerson is so quick to unfurl.

"Now," Sigerson says, "play for me any piece that you like. No Bach, though. I intensely dislike hearing amateurs play Bach. Let me have a waltz."

Such rudeness. I am shocked that Holmes has no rejoinder to make. No, instead he is tucking his fiddle under his chin, and his eyes assume the faraway look that betokens a profound focusing of his mental powers.

His is an altogether danceable rendition of a waltz. I must record that he is rather rising to the occasion. I tap my toe discreetly inside my shoe.

When Holmes finishes, Sigerson says, "Not too bad. You show sensitivity to the musical line."

I see the faintest look of pride cross Holmes's face. "But before we can go on, I must ask you a question," Sigerson says. "We can continue. We can work on this piece and others like it, perhaps something a little more difficult before the Opera Orchestra leaves town—"

"Where do you go next?" Holmes interrupts.

"To Edinburgh," Sigerson replies and waits.

"I might journey to Edinburgh for the sake of a lesson or two," Holmes says politely.

"Really, you are that interested? Then the alternative I was about to propose is the only logical course, but I am anticipating you, and it is most important that this be your own choice."

While he waits for a sign from Holmes, Sigerson's face is full of a strange sincerity. He cares too much about teaching and fiddle music. The intensity is almost pathological.

"Yes," Sigerson continues, "we could simply go on from your present level of accomplishment. The other course we can pursue is to go back to the beginning, to look at the way you hold the bow, to discuss how you change positions on the fingerboard, to analyze your vibrato. In short, to abandon music for mechanics. Yet it will all be for the sake of the music finally."

Holmes responds amicably, "This is no difficult decision. Any intelligent man would prefer to learn the basics correctly. I might be given pause by your statement about mechanics rather than music if I had not heard you yourself play. It is quite certain"—Holmes bows slightly—"that music is always the first consideration for you. You make no merely mechanical sounds."

"I am flattered," says Sigerson as he takes up his own violin. "But before we go back to the beginning, I will show you a few things about this waltz that you have just been so kind as to play for me and Dr. Watson."

Sigerson plays the first phrases of the waltz. I cannot help but see that in his hands it is a piece transformed. When Holmes plays it, I want to dance; when Sigerson plays it, I wish to fly. It is very charming.

"Bravo!" Holmes says, "You have just performed the passage ten times better than I." Holmes is in a wonderful mood.

"Why is it better?" Sigerson says.

"That is something you must tell me," Holmes responds.

"Then watch." He turns to me. "Dr. Watson, in case Mr. Holmes's memory fails, unlikely event, this information should be recorded in your notes along with the information about the colour of my handkerchief."

"I say, how did you know I recorded that?"

"Consider for less than a second," says Sigerson. "I had not said a single thing worth recording, my sneeze was the most dramatic event thus far, and directly after it, you scribbled away. Also, I am well aware that the colour scheme is scientifically combined in such a way as to attract notice."

"Please continue with my lesson," Holmes says politely. "I know that your time is precious."

Here Sigerson takes up his violin again and plays two notes, then pauses with his bow suspended above the strings. "Notice where my bow is," he says. "Here you must lift, really lift. The gesture is very small and yet it must be authentic." He plays the two notes again and then asks Holmes to try it.

"Quite good," Sigerson says, "but not free enough. You must be airborne. True, you are only two centimeters into the air, but it must have the feeling of being really there."

Holmes repeats his attempt.

"Yes, better," say Sigerson, encouragingly. "But the second note does not sail. It is with the second of the two notes that you become airborne. The two notes cannot sound exactly the same."

Again he demonstrates, and it is true that his two notes have a quality that Holmes's entirely lack. Holmes tries again and again. "Listen to it yourself," Sigerson says. "It will improve," and he wanders around the room while Holmes plays the same two notes many times. It is becoming extremely monotonous to my ear, but suddenly Sigerson shouts, "Better, much better. You have an ear as well as an eye, sir. Now the next two notes in the phrase."

It turns out that these new notes are in fact the same as those we have just heard for a prolonged period of time.

"Yes, yes," Sigerson says, for the first time a little impatiently, "but of course one does not just repeat the pattern without *any* variation. Where does that take us? Nowhere. Music never stands still. Certainly not a waltz. Not 'Tales from the Vienna Woods.' Listen."

Again Sigerson plays the entire phrase. Then he asks Holmes what he has heard.

Sounding much like a Gradgrind, Holmes enunciates, "The phrase consists of eight notes, and they are grouped by twos. The first three sets are in fact the same pattern—"

"But," interrupts Sigerson, "though the same notes are repeated, each group is played with increasing intensity, *nicht wahr?* So the music moves forward, and we are entirely ready to make the move up a third to the last two notes. Now play the first six notes, but not the final two. Make me anticipate those two, however; *imply* that they are to come."

Holmes does as he is instructed, and Sigerson says words of encouragement. The youth is a very strict teacher, but it is clear that he has found in the great detective a student ready to receive tirelessly the most minute corrections. I notice that Sigerson has placed my flowers on the bureau beside an open bottle of toothache medicine. The odour of cloves and camphor hangs in the air.

Finally they have gotten all eight notes to a state of near-perfection. I am drowsy. It has taken them forty-five minutes. But when Sigerson picks up the violin and plays them all together, the eight-note phrase is suddenly fresh again, as fresh as the odour of violets in spring.

Then Sigerson allows Holmes to play the next eight notes. He informs Holmes that all sixteen have the shape of a little hill. "A peak of meringue, if you please. It swoops up, and then it must swoop down. And the whole thing is full of air. What is meringue without the support of air?"

Then Sigerson plays both phrases, and as he does he waltzes with his violin gracefully around the room. I am not quite prepared for such an exhibition—his coattails are flying—but Holmes takes it without lifting an eyebrow.

"Would you like to try that way?" Sigerson asks.

"Playing the violin is quite enough to occupy all my attention," Holmes responds.

"But try it, just a little together."

Holmes shoulders the fiddle, and Sigerson faces him like a dancing partner, though he too has his fiddle up. Sigerson moves backwards, and Holmes waltzes toward him. They make only a few steps, with Holmes trying desperately to get the hang of it but really looking quite stiff, when Sigerson breaks it off. "Just play now."

A mere half hour is spent on the second phrase, and then fifteen minutes on the two phrases joined together.

Finally Sigerson puts his hand to his swollen jaw and grimaces. Then he says that they must end the lesson for the day. He tells Holmes to practice the whole piece, applying the principle of forward motion to the rest of it, and then he invites us both to return at the same hour the next day.

As we walk home—I, quite exhausted, Holmes, full of energy—I ask him what is his opinion of Sigerson now?

"A person of intelligence as well as genius," Holmes pronounces. "Would you care to attend the opera tonight?"

Alas, Holmes wishes to have another opportunity to

witness the talents of Sigerson at his place in the violin section of the Munich Opera Orchestra. "I will provide you with a dinner at Simpson's," Holmes adds.

Immediately, I envision us upstairs at Simpson's. A waiter rolls back the gleaming lid of the silver server to reveal a joint of exquisite tenderness. And so, though my head is ringing with two-note phrases, I agree to subject myself to more music in the evening.

"And what of interest did you observe beside the music?" Holmes inquires.

"Merely that he has chosen to live in the dullest hotel room in London. A clothes press, a mirror, a small table and two ladder-back chairs, a bed, wallpaper studded with cabbage roses—nothing at all expressive."

"Most men when travelling do leave this or that around, don't they? I mean things that testify indirectly to their taste and personality."

"All conspicuously absent, I assure you. I had absolutely nothing to do for an hour and a half but gaze at common furniture."

"Watson, you are really invaluable!" Holmes stops our progress down the street in order to shake my hand.

"I really don't know what you mean," I say, trusting in his sincerity nonetheless.

"You said, 'all conspicuously absent.' And that is a positive observation as well as a negative one. What does it tell us? The same thing that his assuming unnecessary eyeglasses tells us. He is making a thorough effort to reveal as little of himself as possible."

I answer, "Then why does he bother to have us about at all?"

"Again, Watson, you ask the precisely relevant question."

We resume our brisk walk down the street.

"I don't wish to sound vain," Holmes begins, "but I think that he is rather fascinated with me. Now, if you have time, let us just step into The King's Spur and make an inquiry or two."

We enter the pub where only lately the extraordinary duel between Lestrade and Sigerson was enacted. Holmes approaches a waiter and after a few pleasantries about how difficult it is to spot foreigners in London today if they are of European origin, Holmes poses a question to the waiter.

"I should think," Holmes says, "that they would come and go as a part of the general crowd. That snooker player, for example, probably has been here several times, perhaps when a number of the men from the Yard were here indiscreetly discussing this or that difficult case? And yet you've never noticed him."

"Oh, not so, Mr. Holmes," say the waiter. "He's been here all right. Didn't hob-nob any with the lads. They took no note, but I did. I looked at his fancy jacket, knew right off he was a Frenchie. No, when you work in a place, you notice."

"So you do," say Holmes in a congratulatory and ingratiating tone. "Of course you wouldn't recall the tenor of the general talk on such occasions."

"Well, with the Yard boys it's either snooker, or the horses, or the cases."

"Imagine that little problem of the identity of the murdered man in Hammersmith came up?"

"Oh, yes, they were hot on that one. Talked it over

every night until Lestrade had it nailed down."

"Lestrade?" I say indignantly, but Holmes quietly squeezes my arm. It was Holmes himself who solved the bludgeoning. He exchanges a few more companionable words with the waiter, and we leave.

Once in the street, Holmes laughs with delight.

"Do you see the point, Watson? What did we learn from our little chat?"

"That Lestrade wishes to appear to be a better investigator than he is or ever will be."

"Of course, but that is not the real point. *Sigerson* is the man in question. We have learned that he has been to the tavern before, and while he was there he has heard how a puzzling case was skillfully solved. Not being a dullard himself, he perceived that not Lestrade but some other hand pulled away the veil, as you writers might put it. And that hand, Sigerson deduced, was my own."

Holmes is full of self-satisfaction.

He goes on, "You posed the question as to why a person who was so cautious about being known would consort with you and me. My hypothesis was that he is fascinated with me. Our excursion into the tavern tends to confirm the hypothesis. He has listened to tales of my power."

This all seems rather far-fetched, and I say so.

"Of all men, Watson, you should not call a fascination with the world's first consulting detective far-fetched!"

I assure him that my interest in his doings has nothing in common with those of the violinist.

"Probably not," Holmes says. "But hold—again you flush the bird for me. You intend to profit from our association—oh, don't misunderstand me. I do not underestimate the quality of friendship that you so generously offer to one who is unworthy of it. But you *have* worked up a story or two based on our association, haven't you? And Sigerson? Yes, he prolongs an association with me for some definite reason. He harbours a reason quite clear to himself, though it is not yet clear to you or me."

"I should think that if he is a person of such superior intelligence that he would see that it is far better simply to tell you outright what he wishes of you."

"It must be a matter of extreme delicacy. You have observed that he has been testing me. First, in the matter of the varnish: he wished to ascertain if I were a competent chemist and if I were honest enough to tell Klaus that the violin was not a Guarnerius. Then he wondered what my attitude toward him would be after he plucked the violin away from me when I had expressed interest in purchasing it. His test in the tavern was partly one of my goodwill and partly one of my intelligence. Of my intelligence he was already fairly certain, as he risked his own performance as a telepathic on my understanding the significance of a single sentence."

"A single sentence?" I question.

"Yes, perhaps you didn't notice."

"What sentence?"

"Oh, you know. The one asking if I were willing to participate in black magic as an antecedent to our convergence of minds." A faint smile dances at the corners of Holmes's grim mouth. "Got it now, Watson?"

"I haven't an inkling of what you're getting at."

"A parlor game, for children, called 'Black Magic.' You simply refer to something black immediately prior to indicating the correct answer. Surely you noticed I put my hand on the *black* curly head of some lad and then pointed to the true owner of the handkerchief?"

I sigh and suddenly feel weary. The mind of Holmes is a labyrinth of such intricacy that he must play Ariadne or I cannot thread my way out.

"What interests me," he continued, "is the risk Sigerson was willing to take. That he would know that I would know a password *must* be given. That he would know that I would not miss the significance of the veiled clue when it *was* given."

I cannot share Holmes's interest in Sigerson. If this were a case that might become the nucleus for a story, then I should apply myself to it with a will. Klaus's petty crime is not worth pursuing, and it has only led us to associate with a violinist.

"You mustn't limit yourself to the sensational," Holmes enjoins, as though he has been following *my* line of thought.

4

A NEW LESSON

IN THE EVENING—it is a delight to walk with a good companion to a good café on a balmy spring night; London is quieter, less restless; one feels that there is no point in further work; there is time to spare before retiring; and it is good not to be alone—Holmes and I enjoy a dinner of kidney pie at The Dog and Shepherd and then head for the opera. I have suggested—or perhaps it was Holmes—that we reserve Simpson's for an evening when we have hours and hours.

We lounge about the entrance to the Opera House because Holmes wishes to watch the dark window of Sigerson's room. We are approached twice by suffragettes who are requesting signatures on their petition, but both Holmes and I politely decline. There is a man among the petitioners—Pankhurst—and Holmes treats him to an icy glare.

"Is it logical," Holmes says to Pankhurst in an acid tone of voice, "to assume that you will gain sympathy by accosting and perhaps embarrassing those of us to whom a delightful evening of music is the main concern?"

"Perhaps people should be embarrassed that women are denied the vote," Pankhurst quietly answers.

"I would advise that you confine yourself entirely to writing letters to the editor of the *Times*. That is the place for rational persuasion, not the opera house. Indeed, if your letters *are* rational—and very few are—they will attract more attention than this spectacle."

Having delivered his opinion, Holmes spins on his heel so that Pankhurst is decidedly dismissed. That gentleman seems to take Holmes's rebuke in stride. Cheerfully, he turns to another couple who approach the entrance with tickets at the ready.

At that moment, Holmes nods towards Sigerson's window, and I note that it is now lighted and Klaus has entered the room. Sigerson and Klaus stand in the window talking; they are close enough to the center of the room so that we can only see their heads above the window sill. But as we watch we see something quite shocking. I wonder if I am mistaken, and I think that I surely must be.

I see, or I think that I see, Sigerson suddenly lean forward and kiss Klaus lightly on the cheek. I would entirely discount the scene as an optical illusion, given the space separating us from them, except for the fact that I feel Holmes's entire body jerk into stiffness. I glance at him, but his face is rigid. He does not take his eyes from gazing at the window. Suddenly the light in the corner room is extinguished.

"Musicians!" I exclaim.

Holmes does not move. I see that he is grievously

affected by the scene. The veins are standing out on his forehead, and I really fear that he will attract attention. He stands grim as an American totem pole.

Soon we see Sigerson and Klaus step from the hotel door toward the Opera House. They are dressed in concert regalia, black tuxedos, and they are carrying their instrument cases. Holmes pulls me aside so that we will not be noticed, but he continues to stare at them with singular concentration. Like blackbirds, a flock of musicians emerges into the street.

The suffragettes present their petitions to the orchestra members just as they have to the early public. Most of the musicians laugh rather rudely; their rosy faces become wreathed in smiles, and their bellies shake under the tuxedos. One twirls his mustache, grabs the pen, and scrawls his name in huge letters across the page, quite ruining it.

We notice that Emmeline Pankhurst—I recognize her from newspaper illustrations of the suffragettes—puts her hand on the sleeve of Sigerson's coat. To our surprise, he covers her hand with his own, and then signs the petition.

Walking on, he calls back to her, "I shall send you a contribution."

"It's very good of you, sir, I'm sure," she replies.

As I look at Holmes I see that his face has relaxed. He has gotten over the shocking display in the hotel window. He is more interested than amazed by Sigerson's exchange with the suffragettes.

I cannot note much about the opera, except that it is another performance of *The Magic Flute*, for I fall asleep soon after it begins. Holmes wakes me up to hear a special part played by the flautist Bachaus, whom Klaus had attempted to impersonate. It is a whistling sort of tune.

In the morning, I doubt that Holmes will wish to return to Sigerson's chamber for another lesson, but I am mistaken. Holmes is up early and waits for me at the door of the apartment, his violin case in hand.

As we walk to Sigerson's, Holmes questions me again on my observations of the day before. Again, I list the common furniture that I observed.

"But what about behaviour, Watson? Now that you think it over, what comes to your mind about his behaviour?"

Holmes's attitude is considerably less cocky today. He seems to be turning over possibilities again and again in his mind. I imagine the process has all the monotony of playing two notes over and over. Earlier he has practiced his waltz for an hour or two, but I noticed that even then he did not concentrate. The music had its habitual overlay of melancholy, as though it were a mere accompaniment to his thoughts. Indeed, I felt like saying at one point, "More airy, lighter! Meringue! Can you not remember your instruction?" But knowing that Holmes was troubled, I had restrained myself.

"Behaviour?" I reply. "He can waltz while he fiddles. Probably he can juggle as well."

Holmes ignores my sarcasm. "Yes, the waltzing," he says meditatively.

As we pass the flower stand, I mention that yesterday Sigerson blithely took the flowers I happened to have purchased.

"Stop," Holmes exclaims. "Would you go back and purchase another bouquet? I should like to see what happens today." He has become rather excited. As I buy a handful of lilacs, I see that Holmes is watching me and pressing his fingertips together. Usually this is a sign of success in his deductions.

Slowly he says, "You know that it is one of my principles that once you have eliminated all the possibilities, then what remains, no matter how improbable, is the truth."

When we arrive at his room, Sigerson haughtily ignores me altogether. He scarcely gives Holmes a civil greeting.

"Let's hear the G-major scale," he says wearily. Not a word about the waltz Holmes practiced all morning. Sigerson stations himself on the other side of the room. Balefully eyeing Holmes, Sigerson reaches in his velveteen jacket for a cheroot. He has a sour, and yet dejected, expression on his face.

I am subjected to the G-major scale as many times as it can be repeated in an hour. Sigerson is certainly intent on shaping Holmes's technique. It is a pure trial. Sigerson himself does not even take out his own instrument until I have endured nothing but Holmes for an hour.

"Watch what you're doing!" Sigerson says sharply to Holmes, whose eye has wandered for a moment. Poor Holmes! He appears positively cross-eyed from looking down the violin at his vibrato. Sigerson gives not one friendly word to him, but puffs on his cheroot. Finally Holmes takes the violin from beneath his chin to rest a moment.

"It would seem," I observe, not having spoken for an hour, "that the G-major scale is rather difficult."

Sigerson fairly barks at me: "*Life* is difficult, and especially playing the violin!"

"I'm sorry to have disappointed you today," Holmes says mildly.

"I *am* disappointed in you," Sigerson says, his grey eyes flashing. "I had taken you for a rational man, but what do I see when I look out my window last night? I see that you refuse to sign the petition for suffrage. I see that you turn your back on a noble gentleman of your Parliament who has ten times the courage that you do!"

Holmes says, "I have not had time to consider the issue. I never act hastily."

"And you shall never have time to consider the issue because you do not make it your business to consider it."

Holmes looks at Sigerson steadily. Around Holmes's thin lips plays a slight smile. I see he is very far from losing his temper and perhaps he is even pleased that Sigerson has allowed himself to register passion. In his most soothing tone, Holmes says, "I give you my word that I *will* consider the issue."

Sigerson's face softens, and the anger melts away.

Holmes goes on in his calming way, "I give you my word to consider it—my word, shall I say, not as a gentleman, but as an aspiring musician."

Sigerson's face assumes a new expression, one of alert curiosity.

"Yes," Holmes goes on, "as an aspiring musician who will do something quite contrary to his natural disposition—Watson can tell you that I have no interest in any political issues—in order that his musical career might proceed in a constructive way."

Abruptly Sigerson turns away. He seems almost confused. He walks automatically to his violin case, unsnaps the locks and says, "Here, let me show you how a scale ought to be played. We'll go around the circle of fifths, in four octaves."

He plays very rapidly and nimbly. As the home note of the scale is reached he emphasizes it before ascending another octave. I must say that I do not care for the highest notes on the violin, even when expertly executed.

I busily store his advice in my notes: "Open the arm at the elbow," Sigerson says as he plays. "Drop your wrist more gradually as you play the downbow; don't arch too soon on the upbow."

After a quarter of an hour, he orders a change in the bowing style. "*Spiccato*," he calls, and the smooth motion of the bow is broken into a scale's worth of little jerks. It turns out that Holmes's *spiccato* is poorly controlled, but now Sigerson is kind in his instructions, and he praises Holmes when he makes slight progress. When the amount of time that we spent yesterday has passed, I cough unobtrusively, hoping to signal them to stop. They both turn their penetrating grey eyes upon me; it is like looking down the barrels of four matching pistols.

But at last the lesson ends. I think that it is only because Holmes takes pity on me.

Before we make our departure, Holmes says, "I must bring up the question of how I can repay you for these lessons. Do you have a regular fee?"

"Yes," Sigerson responds. "I teach in Munich, and I do

have a regular fee, but that is not what I shall charge you."
He hesitates and puts away his violin. He looks mischie-
vously at Holmes. "You yourself will deduce what it is I
wish you to do. Something quite in your line, I might add.
A little piece of detective work. Will you be up to it?"

"I think so," Holmes says.

"I think that you may know it now," Sigerson says
carefully, "but if you have not guessed the nature of the
task in a day, I shall tell you. I shall be leaving for
Edinburgh in a short while."

With that he abruptly shakes hands, first with Holmes
and then with me, something he has never done before.

❧ 5 ❧

VIOLETS

HERE I PAUSED in my reading and closed my marbled notebook to gaze out the window. It was snowing very heavily now, and the sounds of traffic in the street below were muffled. It was as though a shroud of white were being fitted over the city.

The next entry in my old marbled notebook was an exercise in describing how a good dog follows a scent. When a good dog traverses rough terrain, he will wear his nose raw in an effort to find his subject.

But where was I to turn next for a whiff of my subject? I decided to check Holmes's diary, locked in the deal table. But where was the key? I threw myself in a chair next to the fire and stared into the flames. Where was the key to Holmes's most intimate thoughts? My eye fell on the Persian slipper. Its royal purple cover was faded. My eyes followed a brocade arabesque on the toe over and over. Concealed in the lining of the toe? But I did not arise to investigate. I knew that I was incorrect.

As mankind has done since the cave days, I meditated on the dancing flames. Some other private place. The violin case!

Once again I snapped up the locks. The violin looked sad to me, like something coffined. I tilted it up and raised the lid of the compartment that had pillowed its scroll. Then I lifted the plush lining at the bottom of the compartment and there it was—a still-bright key to the drawer of the deal table. It was my own hand that lifted it up, but I envisioned the elegant hand of Holmes holding the key, not afraid to let me see his hiding place, confident of my respect for his privacy.

This gave me pause; what right did I have to read Holmes's diary, surely far more intimate than the commonplace books? But I unlocked the drawer—my fingers trembling—and pulled out the diary.

Immediately under the entry 1886, subdivision April, Holmes had scrawled *"Victor Sigerson, English Violet."* Then he had written the following entry: *"Watson lacks any appreciation of the subtlety of the Victor Sigerson affair. . . ."*

I was not surprised to see this sort of observation written in Holmes's own hand. From time to time, he often spurred himself on by permitting himself to make adverse comments about me. Many times he had said much worse than this to my face. I forgave him when he was alive, and I was not troubled to read this rather abrupt little note in his diary. I continued to read:

> though perhaps it is just as well, since he would have been shocked by the events of the last two days, namely, April 15 and 16, 1886. "Beware the Ides of March," Caesar was

told, but certainly no danger exists in connection with the Ides of April. Had my discovery been dangerous, Watson would have been the very man to have had by my side with his service revolver. . . .

Holmes did display a good deal of gratitude to me on many occasions when we worked together. This sort of off-hand compliment must be taken as the mate to the more left-handed observations.

After attending *The Magic Flute* and tucking Dr. Watson in at Baker Street, I watched Klaus and a triple-chinned friend leave their hotel. What luck! They did not see me, and now I knew his room was empty.

Hotel door locks are surely a joke among hotel management. A child could open one. With the aid of a tiny but sturdy wire, I was in Klaus's room in less time than it would have taken an ordinary person to use a key.

The room had been brutalized by the week-long stay of the musician. One of the mattresses had been thrown onto the floor. Bed pillows (he had apparently insisted on an inordinate number of that item) sat in the chairs. Clothing fit for a circus performer was thrown on the bureau and chest. The mirror had been taken from its holder above the dresser and propped up in a chair at the foot of the bed. The bedposts served as anchors for a cord stretched between them, and on the cord was suspended a row of sausages of various sizes. The place resembled a Bavarian butcher's shop, except for the bedding and clothes, which suggested an Irish laundry.

I stepped carefully through the disarrayed fabrics so as not to disturb them, though I was quite certain that no one would have noticed had I taken a stick and stirred the entire mess. Just as I had anticipated, two large wardrobe closets stood against the wall that separated this room from Sigerson's room. I stepped inside a closet, leaving the door ajar so that the small amount of city light and moonlight that filtered into the room from outside would still be available to me. These hotel wardrobes are built cheaply. The closets lacking any back of their own, the room wall serves as their fourth side.

It was simplicity itself to take a sharp little auger from my pocket and remove a portion of the plaster. The plaster was old and hard and some sound was inevitable, so I was relieved when Sigerson in the adjacent room took out the violin and began to practice the Bach "Chaconne" that had so entranced me the first time I heard its melody floating out the window.

I was careful to make as little noise as possible in any case, but it was indeed delightful to have such marvelous music to listen to while I accomplished this rather tedious task. I turned the auger at the moment that I knew an accent or a loud double-stop would occur in the "Chaconne." Eventually, though, I forgot to bore in and merely listened, mesmerized, till I was lost in the interstices of the single final note.

When a lively "Gigue" followed, I resumed my moonlight work. A crash in the street below interrupted Sigerson's playing. I heard his footsteps cross to the window. During this distraction I was able to bore through a lathe, which was a somewhat noisy job.

Suddenly Sigerson gave a little high-pitched yelp. I feared that I had been discovered.

Instead Sigerson ran out his door without stopping to lock it. (Not a very astute move, considering the presence of the Stradivarius violin. Had I been a burglar I would have counterfeited some such disturbance to get Sigerson to leave the room in a hurry.)

I left the closet to peer through the window, and I saw that a cab conveying Klaus and his triple-chinned companion had been involved in an accident. Klaus seemed to have cut his forearm, which was bleeding profusely.

The sight of the blood had no effect on Sigerson, who was far less squeamish than a number of the men who were already on the scene. Sigerson pulled a large handkerchief from a hip pocket and made a tourniquet of sorts. He also scribbled a note on a piece of paper, apparently sending for a physician.

I knew that they would all shortly come up to the room, but I doubted that my concealing closet would be opened. It contained nothing but spare boots which had recently been rubbed with mink oil. The clothes were strewn about on the floor. So I worked like a beaver and gnawed my way entirely through the wall. I even had time to run into Sigerson's room and to smooth out the edges of the puncture made on his side. Fortunately my spy hole fell in the center of a cabbage rose on the wallpaper, and it would be scarcely noticed. Then, returning to Klaus's wardrobe closet, I knelt among the boots.

As they entered Sigerson's room, I heard him reassuring Klaus and his friend that the wound was not so dangerous as they had first feared. There was no arterial damage. However, a doctor would be coming soon.

I positioned my eye at the peephole, and none other than Dr. Watson, bag in hand, entered my line of vision. Of course Dr. Watson was the only physician whom Sigerson knew. Apparently he had not informed Dr. Watson that it was Klaus who required his services. Being a thoroughly professional man, Watson went to work on his patient. It turned out that the wound was more than superficial, and Dr. Watson executed a number of stitches as skillfully as any woman might mend a rent in a sleeve. After Watson had applied the dressing, I noted that it was Sigerson who insisted on paying Watson, on the spot.

Next, Klaus and the triple-chinned German were escorted back to Klaus's room where I stood silently within the wardrobe. Klaus had a store of wine as well as sausages, and soon they were drinking and eating a few feet from my position. With the sounds of crude chewing and slurping in my ears, I watched quite a different scene through the peephole in the other room.

Sigerson sat limply in a chair. He too seemed to listen—probably for sounds that would tell him Klaus and his friend had retired. Thus sat Sigerson for an hour or so until things grew quieter. Light from Klaus's room rimmed my ill-fitting closet door. I dared not move, and I began to feel a cramp in my calf. Finally Klaus extinguished the bedroom light.

Arranging myself for a more comfortable view through the peephole, I endeavoured to fasten all of my attention on Sigerson, who sat for perhaps another quarter of an hour before making any move to undress. It must have been close to midnight. I judged the time by the church bells that always haunt the London air. Then Sigerson extinguished a light, and the room was plunged into semi-darkness.

The light coming in the window was considerable, though, and I shamelessly watched the violinist remove the velveteen jacket. Next, from the back of a drawer, hidden under several pairs of trousers, Sigerson drew a sleeping garment. It cascaded from the slender hands: a yoked, pleated, and lacy garment such as any woman would like to sleep in. I watched only a moment more for the unbuttoning of the shirt, when I saw exactly the data that I sought.

I averted my eyes, as it was never my intention to penetrate any more of this maiden's modesty than most women display when they attend the opera.

I closed the entry under English Violet with a bang. Imagine that! Sigerson a woman in disguise! And Holmes never bothered to tell me! What transpired next! I re-opened the entry, my eyes racing over the words.

I [Holmes wrote] could have chosen to leave the closet. After all, the loud snoring of the Germans would have masked the creak of any loose board I chanced to tread upon. But I did not want to go. I slumped to the bottom of the wardrobe and lay on my side, curling my knees up to a tolerably comfortable position. Throughout the night, I heard the gentle breathing of Sigerson, like an ethereal descant over the ground bass of the Germans.

Klaus and his friend turned out to be slug-a-beds, and it was mid-morning before they left their room for breakfast, and I returned to Baker street.

"I don't know what you've been doing," Watson said, "but last night I was obliged to make a call I would rather not have made."

"Not on the flute player?" I said.

"Why, yes. How did you guess?"

"Not for an arm injury?"

"You astound me. Which arm?"

"The right. A cut about three inches long on the inside of the forearm."

"You must have witnessed the accident then!"

"I was in the vicinity."

"What else do you know about my escapade?" Watson looked almost frightened. Perhaps I should have had mercy on him.

"Sigerson was kind enough to pay your fee last night," I continued.

"Really, Holmes, how can you have divined that? You're quite right."

"Let me just say that you do not have the irritable manner of a physician who has been obliged to pay a call without receiving his professional due."

"Perhaps I can be spared from being present at your third lesson?" Watson asked in a tentative manner.

Indeed, his absence was essential to my next investigation.

Quickly, I picked up my violin and made my way back to the hotel. I was beginning to feel like something of a resident at those premises. When the door to the corner room, second floor, opened to admit me, at first I saw no sign of my teacher in the chamber. Then the door closed behind me, and of course there she stood behind the door.

The donning of a dress entirely changed her appearance. She laughed and said, "Don't pretend to be surprised, Mr. Sherlock Holmes. You had already guessed my secret, I'm sure."

"Madame, I believe that I had. And you are?"

She nodded politely and smiled, "Violet Sigerson."

On looking into her face, I noted that all the features were familiar. Of course. Only in the context of a dove-grey dress, the delicate jaw and neck appeared appropriate instead of a near abnormality. Also she had abandoned the unneeded spectacles, and the expression of her eyes seemed less stern. The cropped hair was combed quite differently and curled around the face.

"However, I must congratulate you," I said. "I doubt if anyone else in the world would have guessed your secret."

She invited me to sit down, which I did, though being in the hotel room of a maiden without the presence of Dr. Watson made me feel more nervous than I could have anticipated.

"And of course you know the reason for my little disguise."

"There is not a first-rate orchestra in Europe that would allow a woman to belong as a member. Certainly not a German orchestra. It is really quite *outré* that you travel with them."

"Yes. I have been a member of the Munich Opera Orchestra for two years. During an audition, I was able to play behind a screen. The conductor was exclaiming enthusiastically about engaging me until he saw that I was a woman. The next time I auditioned I was in disguise, and that is how I gained my present position."

"Is Munich your native city?"

"I don't think so. I am an orphan, and I do not know where I was born. I grew up in England, in Birmingham, until the age of thirteen, and then I was sent to live with the family of a distant cousin in Munich."

"Klaus, then, is your cousin?"

"That is correct. And of course Karl has been of wonderful assistance to me in keeping my secret from the orchestra. So far he has not even told his friend."

"Yet, I would guess that you are rather generous to Klaus. Twice you have paid his legitimate debts."

Here I must note that she blushed. It was quite surprising. I had forgotten to expect that sort of reaction from her, for in her speech and manner she continued to appear as straightforward and forthright as she had when she assumed the masculine role.

"Now I wonder," she said, "since you have discovered me, will you wish to continue your lessons?"

I hesitated for a moment. Indeed, it was not much to my liking to have a female teacher. I would have found a polite way of declining except that I noticed a very shrewd and judgmental light in her eyes. I did not wish to appear to be quite so irrational as the Munich Opera Orchestra conductor, and so I said, "How else do you expect to pay me for the service that I am about to perform for you?"

She laughed, but then she added a little anxiously, "Of course I could pay you."

"Even after your generous contribution to the suffragettes?"

Again she blushed and said, "Really, Mr. Holmes, I think you must know everything."

I hoped that she did not know that I had watched her disrobe the night before.

"How did you know that I had penetrated your disguise?" I asked.

"Because I made two mistakes, and you noticed them both. First, I received Dr. Watson's bouquet as though I were in my own drawing room. Then when I invited you to try a waltz step, I automatically assumed the position of the woman and moved backwards. You, Mr. Holmes, are a very poor dancer, but I knew that the scene would tease your mind until you had discovered why it seemed strange. Both you and I know that no man will fail to take the lead in dancing. Also, you are such a fastidious observer that you could not merely look at me repeatedly without beginning to wonder about my gender. Yet, because of your own prejudice about women, I truly doubt that your eyes could have told you what your ears insisted could not be true."

"And what prejudice is that?"

"You doubt that any woman can play the violin as well as I do."

I must admit that I had already revised my opinion and decided that I had deceived myself about the quality of the playing. She was my superior and a master-player, but surely I had been mistaken in judging her to be of the genuine virtuoso category of violinists. Yet I did not wish to hurt her feelings by saying so. It was clear that she was a woman of unusual courage, and I quite admired her for it. While I searched my mind for something tactful to say, she interrupted my thoughts.

"Please do not dissemble, Mr. Holmes. It would not be becoming to you. I understand fully what is going through your mind. You are excusing yourself for having overrated me. You are telling yourself that you were eager to have a good teacher and when you heard me playing through an open window on a spring day—why the very air probably distorted the sound. I feel sorry for you, Mr. Holmes, for you are in the bonds of society's prejudice."

This speech was heartfelt on her part. I shrugged and assured her that I knew that there was still much that I could learn from her.

"This will not do," she said. "I will not go forward on these grounds. Instead, you must sit and listen to me play. Close your eyes from time to time, if you like, if *their* evidence disconcert you. As you are an honest listener, Mr. Holmes, I will convince you now not only that I am as good a player as ever you thought me to be, but, indeed, that I am a better player."

"Very well," I agreed. "I shall be honoured to hear you play." But what mettle! I remembered that I had seen her perform under a good deal of pressure when she beat Lestrade at snooker—snooker! A woman expert!—and I began to anticipate that I was going to witness an extraordinary effort.

"I shall be a strict judge," I warned.

Her only reply was to go to the violin case and snap up the locks. Most curious how even this simple gesture was now transformed into something touching. I closed my eyes.

What followed was music of extraordinary harmonic combinations. Later she told me that it was a work composed by the virtuoso performer-composer Eugene Ysaÿe and in fact that it had not been published. The first note was simplicity itself, a low, sweet, and careful note, but one prolonged unduly, I thought, until I recognized the unusual character of the piece in general. The second note, a third higher, was bowed again with that odd yearning sound, but with the third note she picked up a double-stop, and then as the musical line ascended into the higher regions of pitch, each note was coupled to a lower note. These double-stops were not the usual thirds and sixths that make such a pleasant underline for a waltz; instead they were fourths, fifths, and sevenths. This work seemed to have been composed on another planet. I opened my eyes in astonishment at this futuristic progression of tones—the composer, a Jules Verne of music.

Violet Sigerson was as absorbed in the music and as oblivious to me as she had been absorbed in snooker and oblivious to Lestrade. Her bow arm opened with exactly the same authority that I had so admired when I first saw her play, only now it was enclosed in a thin grey fabric of a dress sleeve that ended in organdy cuffs and a small bright black button. The bow bit into the strings as it must if a rich sound is to be produced, and yet the whole effect was so otherworldly that I felt a terrible excitement. All of these strange double-stops were played with unerring accuracy of intonation, and it was the integrity of the pitch that made the work awe-inspiring and mesmerizing rather than laughable. As it progressed, the romantically rhapsodic nature became more evident; toward the end (the piece lasted perhaps eight minutes) it seemed to abandon the future and become more traditional. I saw that she loved this strange music, and I could not deny that the performance was one rendered by an authentic genius.

When she finished, I stood and bowed. "I have never heard the violin played like that before."

She laughed and said, "What measure of praise or condemnation am I to construe from this ambiguous observation?"

"I cannot admire your performance enough."

"Thank you," she said simply. "I know that it was not easy for you to be hospitable to such thoroughly modern music. Ysaÿe's compositions are perfectly suited to the violin as an expressive instrument, are they not? I mean the technical requirements peculiar to the instrument are enwrapped in the total idea of the musical composition."

"Are you acquainted with this Ysaÿe?"

"I've seen him in Brussels. Do you wish me to play

something else for you? You would find the compositions of Vieuxtemps more congenial, probably."

"I should like nothing better than that you devote the time you have allotted for my lesson to performing."

She said, "We have not spoken of the reason that I have had need of a discreet consulting detective."

"I have deduced it easily enough. It is your mental habit to inquire after the origins of things. If you are going to purchase a violin, you wish to know its derivation. You spoke of the fact that you are an orphan who spent your early life in England. While you are on tour in England, it is logical to assume that you would like to initiate an investigation into your own origins."

"Yes. If I could appear on my own behalf, I would do it."

"I doubt that it will take more than a few days."

Suddenly another instrument case caught my eye, its snub nose peeking out from under the bed.

"What is that?" I said, pointing.

She retrieved the case, and took out a strange instrument. I saw it was a member of the viol family, one sometimes played by Leopold Mozart, but almost never used in modern times. "The English Violet," I said. I asked myself why she wished to play this now-antiquated instrument. I was surprised to hear myself answering my own question aloud: "Perhaps you have made the instrument a hobby because it shares your name?"

She did not respond in words, but tucking the Violet under her chin, Miss Sigerson played a mellow run. It was a softer instrument than the violin, with an affecting tone. She looked quite the picture of womanly sweetness.

The scroll, carved in the shape of a woman's face and hair, reminded me of a ship's figurehead. The muted runs and arpeggios launched me on a calm sea. Mere exercises, but so soothing that I was sorry when she stopped to talk.

Standing the English Violet on her knee for a moment, she pointed out the extra set of sympathetic strings that are positioned under the fingerboard. They are not directly bowed, but vibrate by sympathetic resonance and thus enrich the tone of the instrument and lend it its peculiar quality.

Having introduced me to the instrument, she resumed playing, and her music—a real piece now—made me strangely restless. I felt a great need to look out the window. But the street was dull with carriages, and nothing outside interested me. Her music drew me to look inward again. Her face was turned from me, and I felt an impulse to touch her hair! I trembled like the sympathetic strings on the viol.

The melody Violet was drawing from the strings recalled the cooing of mourning doves. When I was a child, I sometimes lay in bed in the morning and listened to the doves who nested under the eaves. In her sound and in theirs was something inexpressibly sad that gave companionship to a feeling deep within myself. And yet I was exhilarated!

Then the cooing of the doves was mixed with my mother's humming as she came up the stairs. She was bringing me toast and tea on a tray, and she was going away that day. I can't recall for what reason. Perhaps I was four or five. Two large trunks stood upright at the bottom of the stairs. The day before, I had considered concealing myself in one of them so that I might go with her.

When Violet finished, I mentioned, as calmly as I could, that the Joachim Quartet was in London for its annual performance, and since I had rather overly prevailed on Dr. Watson of late that I should be happy to call on her.

I saw the flash of her eyes, I'm sure of it. But she composed herself and said, "I should not be able to leave the hotel in feminine dress."

"Of course not," I reassured her. (Just as well Watson and the world should always know her as Victor.)

I shall never forget the honest way her eyes met mine when I said, "The English Violet is also called the *Viola d'Amore*."

6

MAGIC

FULL OF WONDER, I slowly closed the entry under English Violet. How he wrote about her! I myself could scarcely have done more justice to feminine charm! Yet, many and many a time, I had recorded his utter indifference to the fair sex.

Feminine charm! Actually she was tall and rather broad-shouldered. Certainly she had the carriage of a man. I thought of how she dominated the snooker table. How, angry with Holmes, she stood at her window smoking a cheroot. Certainly male lungs. There was something hard in her face: probably she had practiced the demeanor of a man in front of a mirror. Her gait was certainly masculine, but then her frock coat always covered the pelvis. And her authority when she played the fiddle! Totally the air of a master. Not being beautiful, in any conventional sense, surely helped to carry it off.

What else might have happened between Holmes and Violet Sigerson? How many chapters in Holmes's life had been entirely buried for years? I wanted to know—not as a potential biographer, but, by Jove, as his trusted companion.

In some agitation I paced around the old digs. It was almost as though Holmes had been unfaithful to our friendship. Nonsense, I told myself. Had I not deserted him to marry, and more than once? At least that was all public and aboveboard. He fully knew what I was up to. Then I calmed myself. It was not as though he had married the woman. Indeed, there was a reluctance to take her femininity into consideration. Most of the admiration was focused on her performance on the violin.

Quickly I turned the page for the next entry in Holmes's diary:

> V. Sigerson, Magician Extraordinaire, Edinburgh
> For an amusing misperception see Watson's speckled travel journal.

"Amusing!" I was miffed. I threw a log on the fire.

The speckled notebooks were rather a misstep, as I recalled. Holmes had suggested that I practice my writing by chronicling his travels. I had found the experiment too dull to continue. But after all, in his personal diary Holmes had relied on my account and written nothing himself.

I knelt before the cabinet housing our journals, some bound in buckram, some paper boards, ah! speckled covers. Well, I would rely upon the speckled notebook, too.

Once inside the stiff covers I quickly found a reference to *"Edinburgh: A Train Trip"*; the entry was studded with allusions to the violinist. I read my own ancient notes:

Holmes has proposed an excursion to Edinburgh. I ask why in particular he wishes to visit that gloomy northern city, when spring has just come to London. He replies that nothing of interest is occurring in London. Ah, Holmes, when will you learn the joys of the change of season? He means, of course, that no client has presented himself of late and that no crime has been referred to him by Scotland Yard.

Well, why not go to Edinburgh? The Queen has her Scottish retreat at Balmoral. Many of us in London who formerly would have taken no interest in that dour land or people are now flocking there as if the scent of highland heather were a necessity of life.

As we board the train at Charing Cross, I note that the whole German outfit is going aboard. My patient, the flautist Klaus, has his arm in a rose-and-grey paisley silk sling.

"What a fondness for silk these gentlemen have," I say with distaste.

"They model themselves after Richard Wagner," Holmes explains. "The walls of his room in the Briennerstrasse in Munich are said to be hung with yellow silk." I cannot help but be excited by the confluence of trains in the station. Their power and size, the clouds of steam arising around them make me think of dragons.

"Total decadence," I say. "The closer we get to the end of the century, the more it is evident that civilization is decaying."

"Wagner's colours," Holmes goes on, "include white, rose, and grey. He had artificial roses all about him in his Munich rooms. They say that soft colours and pleasing scents were necessary for the proper workings of his highly complex mind."

"I shall never again complain of the odour of shag and pungent chemicals in Baker Street," I exclaim, as we board the train.

"Fortunately," Holmes proclaims loftily, "my response to a musician has nothing whatsoever to do with his nature so long as I am listening to the music. Music, like mathematics, is a pure realm in itself and the person of those who provide it for us is an unfortunate encumbrance which all true music lovers do well to ignore."

Seeing that Holmes is in one of his more didactic frames of mind, I resolve to draw his attention to the countryside through which we are passing as the train hurries north, but as I should have known, nature provides little distraction for him.

After we stop at a small station, our compartment is invaded by a family who have neglected to reserve a compartment of their own. They have several children in tow, and ordinarily Holmes would find such an arrangement most disagreeable. As it turns out, the absent-minded gentleman with the long flowing beard is Sir Leslie Stephen. Holmes has heard of his project of editing the great *Dictionary of National Biography*, and they fall into a happy discussion of such work.

"Only the dead to be included," Holmes says approvingly. "Quite right. Think of the squabble that would follow if you allowed the living to be considered."

Sir Leslie Stephen's wife, despite her pregnant state, is exceptionally beautiful, as are the three daughters, Stella, Vanessa, and a chubby girl of four named Virginia.

Vanessa has been provided with a little notebook. With her mother's encouragement, she is drawing a border of flowers around the edge of the page.

"Show Dr. Watson your work," the mother says gently, in the most beautiful of voices.

The little Vanessa turns through the pages of the notebook where she has drawn decorative borders, each composed of stylized flower shapes. The mother also talks gently to each of the other children, especially a lad named Thoby. Virginia stares with eyes round as pennies. Sir Leslie and Holmes, who are deep in esoteric conversation, ignore the children and Mrs. Stephen. I feel a bit sorry for Mrs. Stephen, whose pregnancy surely makes travel less than comfortable.

When I make some remark about their destination, she says that they always move the entire household to the seashore when they can, that it provides a better atmosphere for her husband. We medical men who have to help women through childbirth are sometimes tempted to accuse these progenitors of huge families with selfishness.

It happens that Sigerson comes to the compartment door and knocks. Holmes introduces Sigerson as a musician.

"Papa," Virginia put in, "is he a *magician* or *musician?*"

Here Sir Leslie casts a disapproving glance not at his daughter but at his wife, who has allowed his daughter to interrupt an adult conversation, as if *she*, sweet lady, could have prevented that nonchalant child.

Sigerson quickly says, "Some of both," speaking directly to Virginia. With that he reaches into his pocket and brings out a pfennig which he holds in his hand for a second and then causes to disappear. All of the children say, "Ah!"

Of course I have seen these stunts before.

"Do you mind, Dr. Watson?" Sigerson asks me, politely.

"Not at all," I begin to say, but scarcely are the words out of my mouth before Sigerson has seemed to discover a red ball in the air before my lips.

"A cherry!" Virginia shrieks.

"Quite inedible," Sigerson replies to her, smiling. He has a pleasant way with children. He seems a bit childish, perhaps, himself.

At his fingertips, two blue balls materialize before my eyes.

Virginia says, "How large a ball can you make appear?"

Sigerson looks at her keenly, "Why do you ask?"

The child answers, "I would like to hold a ball the size of the world in my hand."

I chuckle, but Sigerson answers respectfully, "Perhaps you might someday. In your own way."

The children are bouncing in their seats; they are so delighted. Mrs. Stephen laughs in the jolliest way. Sherlock Holmes appears pleased, too. Only Sir Leslie Stephen looks as though he would like to say, "Humbug!"

Then Sigerson pitches a ball up in the air, catches it and then shows his empty hand—the ball has disappeared. Down his sleeve I have no doubt, but he repeats this trick several times and none of us is quick enough to see where he is hiding the balls. Then he points toward Mrs. Stephen's knitting bag on the seat beside her and asks if he may look there for the missing balls which the air seems to have eaten.

"Of course," she says, her face shining, and she hands

him the tapestry satchel. He opens the bag (above the level of our eyes, I note), rummages there, and then holds the bag down for the children to look inside. We see three bright and shining balls.

"They're in a yarn nest," Virginia says, "Like eggs of a jungle bird."

Sigerson plucks out one of the balls and hands it to Virginia. "Remember me."

Mrs. Stephen speaks in her gracious voice, "Sir, you have been so kind. Thank you."

"Perhaps you would like to see my magic show in Edinburgh?"

Mrs. Stephen glances anxiously at Sir Leslie, who is oblivious to her and their brood.

"I'm afraid we must not be delayed in reaching the seacoast," she says.

Virginia looks into Vanessa's eyes and says to her older sister, "I should very much like to have gone, wouldn't you, 'Nessa?"

Abruptly Holmes turns his face to us. "What a perceptive child," he remarks. "At least you and I, Dr. Watson, shall have the pleasure of attending. That is, Herr Sigerson, if your invitation is a general one."

This revue is held in St. Andrew Square, Edinburgh, April 19, 1886. From my vantage point, the stage is dwarfed by the rough terrain that hovers above the city—Castle Rock and the extinct volcano, Arthur's Seat.

Holmes asks me to take notes on the show in which Sigerson and Klaus perform, as magicians.

"Why do they want to do this?" I ask.

Holmes answers, almost angrily, "Klaus constantly presses Sigerson for money. It's tantamount to black-mail."

"Blackmail? Do explain."

"Later, my dear fellow, much later."

It is a colourful crowd, and I recognize tartans of Stewart, Gordon, and McCammon. The night being rather chilly, I wish I had one of their blanket-like plaid mantles.

The whole outdoor occasion has a certain wild and unsettling quality about it. The night is very black, and the gloomy Scottish mountain hovers over us. In con-trast, the stage is glaringly bright, and light diffuses from it into the grassy area where the spectators sit or lounge. The open-air seems menacing to me—perhaps because of the chill.

We watch several acts, but, at length, Sigerson and Klaus appear on a platform overlooking a large vat of water. The stage lanterns reflect off Sigerson's costume, which is all of white satin with a billowing shirt bedecked with a fluffy collar hanging almost to his waist. The trousers are also loose and puffy, drawn in at the ankles and then ruffled again. Klaus wears a tight-fitting diamond-patterned costume of all colours.

A box big enough to hold a person is carried onto the stage and positioned on the platform. The box is perfo-rated like a Swiss cheese.

Klaus holds up a large lock for all to see. He says, "My friend will go into the box, I will lock the box, and the box will be lowered into the water." At this point someone in the audience raises up his own lock and key and insists that it too be added to the steel loop that will secure the door.

Klaus tries to refuse to add this new and unknown lock. However, Sigerson signals the skeptic from the audience to come forward. The burly Scotsman passes the lock to Sigerson, who efficiently examines it. Then Sigerson nods to express his permission that this lock be used.

"I confess," Holmes says, "that I would not allow such a lock. The inner mechanism may have been frozen or tampered with."

Klaus announces, "Into the water, he will go." He stoops and splashes the water about. "How? Tied? Very well, tied." The water tank has a glass panel built into its side, so the audience can see into it.

Klaus secures Sigerson's hands behind his back with several knots. It seems a bit French—as though Sydney Carton were facing the guillotine. The blackness of the sky makes me feel that the Divine has closed his eyes on us and our petty show.

Holmes comments, "Of course it is not much trouble for a good magician to squirm out of any set of knots. I have some skill at this myself."

Sigerson climbs inside the perforated box, and Klaus secures the two locks. Then Klaus and another assistant lower the box into the water. There is no doubt that water invades the box. Through the glass, I see the ruffles on Sigerson's clown costume floating up.

"Poor Sigerson," I say, sympathetically.

"Sigerson is a person of extraordinary nerve," Holmes says admiringly. "Yet I wonder if he is flirting with self-destruction."

"Do you suppose he could drown?" I ask in a practical vein.

"It is usual in such tricks for the water vat to be instantly shrouded so that the magician can immediately begin his escape maneuvers."

A troupe of Scottish bagpipes begins to wail funeral music. The tank is not hidden from public view and Sigerson sits still, under water.

"Like some exotic sea-flower. Petals swaying in the current," Holmes muses.

I confess that I have an increasing urge to interfere.

Holmes continues, "What a waste it would be if the most talented violinist of a generation were allowed to drown."

I begin to note the passage of time with my watch. A full minute wears on as the bagpipes keep up their steady drone. The children in the audience fidget. One of them tugs on his mother's sleeve and asks if the show is over. Two minutes pass, and it is clear that Sigerson has not begun to loosen the knots on his hands, let alone to pick the two locks that hold the box door shut.

"It is entirely possible for these tricks to misplay," Holmes says.

"Klaus is there. He won't let his pal drown," I put in.

"My dear Watson," Holmes says, "you would never allow *me* to drown. But you little suspect how indifferent most people are to the safety of their friends."

A drape is erected. Again I keep track of the time. Klaus stands to one side of the drape, but we are gazing anxiously at the stage.

Now Sigerson has been underwater for a total of four minutes. Some of the ladies seem chilly and a breeze lifts their lace collars and cuffs. A snare drummer begins to sound a tattoo. Like a volley of continuous bullets, the noise is designed to rattle the nerves of the audience.

"Sigerson has been underwater for five minutes." Holmes continues, "Of course, he cannot be holding his breath at all. He has some breathing device, probably a tube to the surface."

At that instant, the drape falls from its rod and Sigerson, dripping wet, stands on the platform beside the vat. The crowd hoots in approval.

I exclaim, "Why, he looks like some helpless animal. A seal more than a human being." His hair is plastered to his skull and his whole face looks flushed and strained.

"Come along, Watson," Holmes says, grimly. "I am determined to speak with Sigerson and Klaus."

The performers' tent area is cordoned off, and an attendant keeps watch there. A brisk Scottish wind, smacking more of winter than spring, blows against us.

I comment that Sigerson's dunking may cause him an illness with the chill wind.

"I hope you're wrong," Holmes replies.

The wind flaps the canvas of the tents. Eventually Sigerson emerges dressed in the dark green corduroy jacket of the dandy's cut that he usually wears. Klaus is walking beside him. Sigerson blows his nose. We hear only a bit of the conversation, but it is clear that Klaus is making an urgent demand for money.

"I promised Schmidt," Klaus explains, "and he'll go with Bachaus if I don't take him out. You simply must have some money about you."

"I made a donation back in London," Sigerson replies.

"What!" Klaus says, and takes Sigerson by the shoulders. Klaus begins to shake Sigerson, when Holmes steps out of the shadows and grabs Klaus. With a single blow Holmes knocks him to the ground. Holmes pounces on the flautist, seizes his lapels, and drags him upright to his feet.

"What? What's this," Klaus says. "The great consulting detective has come to play the role of bodyguard?" He turns to Sigerson, "How dare you! How dare you share our secret?"

"Indeed, sir," Holmes says coldly. "How dare you? You are a man totally debased. It is a criminal act for you to abuse your associate who has risked life and limb for your pocket-money."

"Now is it really, Mister Holmes?" he has the effrontery to say. "And where is my pocket money? In *your* consulting pocket?"

I suspect Holmes would have beaten him unmercifully, except for the fact that Sigerson steps between them.

"Please," he says, "my friend's arm is not healed. I fear that you'll cripple him."

Holmes roars at Klaus, "Sigerson is not to try these dangerous tricks again. Ever. You, sir, shall be accountable to me if even the slightest injury is ever sustained. You will *never* exploit him again."

I have not witnessed Holmes in such a passion!

Sigerson begins to cough, and I can see at a glance that the excitement is not good for him.

"Holmes," I interject, "Sigerson is ill."

Holmes releases Klaus, who runs off to join his friends. Sigerson calls, "Karl, look in your pocket!"

We see Klaus reach in his jacket as he runs, obviously finding some money to his liking and giving us all a farewell wave.

"Would you see me to my room, Holmes?" Sigerson says. He is limp as a girl and trustingly places his hand on Holmes's arm.

Holmes removes his hand, but he seems not at all offended. We begin to thread our way around the tents.

"Now," Holmes says, "I will deduce how you performed the underwater trick, but you must tell me if I am correct. You did hold your breath for two minutes as the audience watched." When we step out from the shelter of the tents, Sigerson begins to shiver. Holmes is relishing his deductions and continues. "Once the drape was in place you simply engaged a flexible breathing tube that was hidden amongst the folds of your clown's collar. It doubtless had a cork attachment so that when you released the tube with your teeth, it floated to the surface."

"Remarkable," I insert.

"Thus you were able to breathe while you used the usual methods to loosen your bonds and then pick the locks."

Sigerson is not breathing comfortably now. He coughs and looks flushed. He says, "I must admit, Mr. Holmes, that you are entirely correct. I am fortunate that the whole world cannot see so easily through my shabby tricks."

"On the contrary," Holmes reassures him. "They require

enormous skill, and even more, they require courage. Should you lose your bite on the breathing tube, you would come close to drowning before your assistant could rescue you."

"I almost *did* drown once," he confesses. "The water must be still, or it will invade the breathing tube. In Amsterdam, someone brought three elephants onto the backstage. Their weight made the boards jounce and that agitated the water. I nearly strangled."

"Did Klaus haul you out?" I ask.

"No. I still had a little air, and I was able to use it to expel the water from the tube, and then breathe again."

Neither Holmes nor I comment, but we both know the terrible self-possession it requires to expel one's last reserve of air at such a moment.

"Now I make certain that nothing shakes the vat of water," he adds. "How did you guess that I had a breathing tube concealed on my person?"

"A magician's costume is usually utilized in his act in some way," Holmes says. "Hence it was easy, once I had observed your voluminous and ruffled blouse, to deduce how it might be used in this particular trick."

"The pagliacci outfit has another use, Mr. Holmes."

Holmes remains silent. Before Sigerson can explain, we turn and enter the Hotel Kenilworth.

7

THE CHOCOLATE NOTEBOOK
AND A HOLE IN MEMORY

THIS WAS THE end of the notation. Ah, Holmes, my friend, you were bitten! Whether you knew it or not, you had gone beyond your role as consulting detective! Your heart had been touched.

I sat and looked around the old digs. Indeed, why had not these rooms, or better rooms, ever been shared by the detective and a wife? I could easily see from my vantage point, decades later, that Holmes was beginning to fall in love, but could he see it then? Did he know where his love of music was taking him?

I spent a full hour rummaging amongst the books, till I found the next link in the chain. It was in my old chocolate-coloured notebook, one devoted to *The Curious Behaviour of Patients.*

At one time, Holmes had thought me best-suited to writing up articles for *Lancet* or the *British Medical Association Journal.* He thought that if I published articles on medical subjects it would have the economic benefit of increasing my practice. Perhaps it would have, but I always had more interest in writing up the human side of my patients rather than their illnesses. I picked up my notebook, carried it to the low chair beside the fireplace, opened the chocolate covers and began to read. At least, when ruminating on "the curious behaviour of patients," I had given up the dreadful experiment of writing in the present tense.

Today I planned to leave Edinburgh, a chilly spot indeed for a holiday, and return to London, the land of lilacs! But! Holmes came into my hotel room, said that he had been around to see Victor Sigerson, and that the lad was quite ill.

Of course I would not dream of refusing to see someone who was ill. Holmes feared that it might be pneumonia. Still the professional call interrupted my plans to leave the city, and so I was in a particularly business-like mood when I approached my patient.

He did, indeed, look ill. Face pale except for red eyes and nose. Voice rendered abnormally high. Fever of 101. Dewy forehead. But, when I proposed to take out my stethoscope and listen to the patient's heart and lungs, he flatly refused. Near-terror filled his eyes.

"Can you not skip this measure in the diagnosis?" he asked feebly.

"Why, I should consider myself negligent if I did," I said.

"Please, Victor," Holmes said anxiously, "Dr. Watson

is a man of utmost discretion. He can be trusted. I myself will leave the room, of course."

"No, no" said Sigerson, fretful as a child. "Too many people already know."

"Hush then," Holmes said sternly, and he tried to take me aside.

"Don't you tell him," Sigerson called. "Don't leave the room with him."

"Act like a man," I told Sigerson sternly. "There's nothing at all to fear about this procedure. Goodness, I cannot believe that you have never had your chest listened to before." I waved the funnel-shaped stethoscope in the air. Sigerson was clutching the covers up to his chin and rolling his head on the pillow.

"Victor," Holmes said soothingly. "Poor Victor," he said and actually smoothed Sigerson's forehead with his hand. I had never seen Holmes assume a bedside manner before.

"Now listen carefully," Holmes said to the patient. "Dr. Watson will not be shocked. He will go along with your little whim, and you will not mind what I tell him."

Sigerson merely stared at Holmes with feverish eyes.

Then Holmes went on, "It seems that Victor has a terrible scar on his . . . chest, don't you Victor?"

The patient nodded.

"He does not wish you or anyone else to see it. He got it in a very foolish way, and he vowed solemnly to the Virgin Mary, for he is a Catholic, that no man should ever see this wound or its scar and sympathize with him over it. Hence, my friend, would you make it possible for your patient to keep his vow by closing your eyes while you listen to his chest? Let Dr. Watson direct you in moving the instrument about, Victor. Would you not permit that?"

Victor said in a pitiful voice, "Is Dr. Watson really to be trusted?"

I should have been offended, but he sounded so weak and at our mercy that I took pains to reassure him. My eyes would be squinched shut. Holmes left the room.

Thus I was allowed to listen to my patient's chest. Upper respiratory congestion. I prescribed absolute bed rest, hot soups, quinine, and powders of acetylsalicylic acid.

Hence the curious behaviour of Victor Sigerson: a man to whom a scarred portion of the body had become a sort of holy shrine. The vows and secrets of patients must be learned if . . .

Here I laughed out loud at my former ignorance. I wondered if all the observations in the chocolate-covered notebook on *The Curious Behaviour of Patients* were based on similar misunderstandings of the true situation. Scars on the chest, indeed! And how Holmes shielded the fair Violet from discovery! Ah, yes, Holmes, you were in love, absolutely in love—whether you knew it or not. The wonder is that I did not see through your silly prevarication on the spot! But why hadn't they trusted me? Holmes trusted me in a thousand cases where indiscretion would have been far more disastrous—not that I was ever indiscreet.

I puzzled over this a bit, and I decided that it was because Holmes's heart was involved that he had not thought so clearly in the matter as usual, or he would have certainly taken me into his confidence.

Could my attacker have been Victor, or rather Violet, Sigerson? Nannerl was not so tall as I remembered Violet/Victor being. But age shrinks us all. I thought of Nannerl's eyes—grey, penetrant, shrewd. They had seemed familiar. Yes, that familiarity had teased my memory: Nannerl *was* Victor Sigerson. Violet Sigerson. She had to be. Had Violet Sigerson spurned Holmes's love?

I threw myself out of my chair and stormed around the room. Why would Violet want to harm me now? Her privacy? His? Could a woman have done such violence to Toby? When I heard a timid knock at the door, I growled, "Come in!" With a good bit of scraping, I pushed away the furniture barricade.

The door opened hesitantly to reveal Mary.

"Sorry to disturb you, sir, but it's afternoon, going on Christmas. 'Ere's a nice rarebit." She removed the napkin from the dish on her tray: a boat of savoury cheddar over bacon and toast. "I'll be going 'ome now. Mrs. 'udson thought I should ask if there's anything else you'll be wanting."

"Kind of you to inquire. Thank you, but this will be all."

She silently disappeared. Too late, I murmured, "Merry Christmas." I neither locked nor barricaded the door.

The rarebit was too hot to eat.

It was still snowing, and a nasty wind was slinging the snowflakes against my window. As I watched the street below, Mary stepped through the front door, and leaned

her tam into the wind-driven snow. Her graceful figure—
she could have been any young woman—seemed sweet to
my eye.

Holmes in love! I thrust my hands in my pockets, and
when I did I discovered a hole with my right index finger.
I was greatly irritated, as one often is by small things when
much larger issues are depressing oneself.

But almost at the same moment, or perhaps just after
my finger jabbed my leg through the opening, I recalled
what was wrong with my whole chain of thought. Victor
Sigerson was dead!

Yes, he had died soon after the events about which I
had just read. And I had written the story myself. It was the
matter of King Ludwig II of Bavaria. I had called it "The
Adventure of the Mad King."

It had never been published. Was it that Holmes did
not want me to publish it? I could scarcely remember. I sat
down to the rarebit. Freckled with a dash of paprika, the
cheese was creamy and flavourful. I remembered with
what difficulty I had persuaded Holmes to allow me to
publish "The Five Orange Pips." That was a painful story
for him because it recorded the unfortunate death of
Holmes's client, John Openshaw of Horsham. Yes, "The
Mad King" was another story that recorded one of our
failures. It was not a failure that haunted me (I cared more
for my patients than for heads of state)—but what had it
meant to Holmes?

I had a comprehensive file of all my unpublished
stories. Of course when I penned this chronicle, I would
have been firm in my assumption that Victor Sigerson was
the male he pretended to be. His voice was convincingly

masculine, his hooked nose carried no hint of feminine pulchritude. I remembered his long, confident stride as he crossed the threshold of the London tobacco shop. In his hotel room, Sigerson had been the master instructor, commanding Holmes to repeat phrases from "The Vienna Woods." Holmes had readily complied. How Sigerson stood before us, violin under his chin, bowing like a prince! Naturally when I wrote about Bavaria I would have assumed without question that the violinist was a man.

I opened the cabinet drawer and eagerly drew out "The Adventure of the Mad King."

III

THE ADVENTURE
OF THE MAD KING

❧ I ❧

TO TRAVEL OR
NOT TO TRAVEL

On a desperately hot day in early June of 1886, Mr. Sherlock Holmes and I sat reading in our Baker Street rooms. Occasionally one of us would simply fold the newspaper and use it as a fan. Over my protest, Holmes prepared for himself another injection of cocaine.

"Soon I shall simply imagine myself to be sitting in a snow drift," Holmes said, rolling up his sleeve.

"I see here," I said, referring to an article, "that Ludwig II of Bavaria has covered an acre with salt. He pretends that it's snow."

"That's a luxury I can scarcely afford," Holmes said.

For two weeks, Holmes had been in a most lamentable state of boredom and depression. Several clients had presented themselves during this time, but he had waved them all away. I had somewhat enlarged my circle of patients, but I knew that Holmes's finances must be in a deplorable state.

In an attempt to delay, if even for a few moments, the

plunge of the hypodermic into his forearm, I remarked, "When you were in Munich, in May, you must have met some people of exceptional interest."

Holmes's eyes narrowed. "Yes. One. A boy of seven named Albert."

I hoped to draw Holmes into a narrative and inquired how his path had crossed the lad's.

"He was also a violin student," Holmes replied testily.

"A prodigy?"

"Not at all. His interest to me was entirely intellectual. He had a compass, Watson. He asked me to explain the force that caused the needle to point north."

"Magnetism," I answered.

Holmes turned from me disdainfully. "Everyone knows that," he said. "But offer an analysis, my dear fellow, of what magnetism is."

"I'm afraid I can't."

"Neither could I," Holmes said, gloomily. "Nor can anyone else. But the boy asked about it."

I sighed. The most trivial questions sometimes hook tenaciously in Holmes's attention.

"Little Einstein has the most determined and objective mind that I have encountered in any Continental country or Great Britain," he said quietly.

Munich was clearly not the subject to enliven Holmes, so instead I directed his attention to Baker Street below our window. "What can you tell me of the people here?" I asked. Actually, there was only one person to be seen below.

"A horseman, I should say by his gait and his clothes," Holmes observed. "And a foreigner. The expensive leather case he is carrying suggests he has considerable resources. Hold, Watson, he has a slip of paper with an address." Usually these anxious glances from address card to door numbers heralded the approach of a client.

"Ah, then," I said lightly, "perhaps you had better hear his story before you go on with your injection."

Holmes shrugged. "Since it is your wish, my dear fellow. But I warn you, I shall not be distracted by any petty appeal for a service that could just as easily be rendered by Lestrade."

Distracted from what? I wanted to ask. *From your own ruin?* Holmes rolled down his shirt sleeve and returned the needle to its small, plush-lined case.

Soon enough, a middle-aged gentleman asked which of us was Mr. Holmes. He spoke with a German accent. His hair was black and combed straight back from his forehead. Perhaps because it was somewhat long, he appeared ill-kept. And his swarthy face was lined in a way that suggested dissipation. Yet the caller possessed a very civil manner.

"My name is Hornig," he told Holmes, "from Oberammergau."

"Ah, yes," said Holmes, apparently recognizing his name. "You have long been the friend of your King Ludwig II, but out of favour now for several years. I believe that I read in the *Times* that His Majesty has suggested that you be given the part of Judas in the Oberammergau Passion Play."

"Yes," said Hornig, smiling somewhat grimly. His teeth were stained in a disgusting way. "His Majesty *has* come to regard me as a traitor, but he is mistaken in this. I was his companion for eighteen years, and though he has turned away from me for the company of younger men, I am actually one of his few remaining friends."

"A man who undertakes to turn summer into winter may be expected to turn friends into enemies," Holmes observed.

"I am still very concerned about the King," Hornig said, and then he glanced at me and hesitated.

Holmes said, "Speak freely in front of Dr. Watson. He is my most trusted colleague and friend."

"This is a matter concerning the first prince of Europe," Hornig objected. As I studied his face, I could see that he might do very well in the unflattering role suggested by Ludwig.

"Tell us why you are here, or leave," Holmes said firmly. "It's all the same to me." And he sighed, eager to employ his own method of turning summer into winter.

"You leave me no choice," Hornig said. "Bluntly put, I wish to engage your services."

We sat down, and with a flick of his hand Holmes indicated to Hornig that he was to present the problem.

"Perhaps you have heard of the King's passion for building," Hornig began. "Soon after he became king— and he was a very young king, eighteen and so handsome that the people all but worshipped him, luxurious brown hair, so thick, that floated about his shoulders like—"

"We have seen pictures of the Swan-Prince," Holmes interrupted. "Pray continue with a description of his building program."

Hornig shot Holmes a glance so full of malevolence

that I was stunned. Holmes merely pressed the tips of his fingers together and sat indolent and relaxed, with his feet outstretched.

"On the third floor of the Residenz, in the heart of Munich, he had an artificial lake constructed. He had a gondola fashioned in the shape of a swan—a Lohengrin motif. The colour of the water could be changed with lights. An invisible orchestra serenaded us while we floated on the lake."

"Pardon me," I said. "But are we really to understand that this lake was constructed indoors?"

"For privacy, you know, and the plants were so fragile. Oh, the burghers knew about it. They were pleased to have so unusual and charming a prince."

"But not so pleased, of late?" said Holmes.

"Well, there were many other projects. Neuschwanstein, you know, dedicated to Wagner."

"I've seen it from a distance," Holmes said. "White and turreted, it rises from the mountain mists."

"After Neuschwanstein, there was Linderhof. It was really *my* favourite. After we were at Versailles we thought we'd have something along those lines—very much in the French style. He's very fond of Marie Antoinette, you know. Something along the lines of her Petit Trianon, where she played at being a shepherdess. At Linderhof, we played. I was made Master of the Horse . . ."

Here Holmes and I simultaneously cleared our throats. It was really a repulsive sight to see the swarthy, middle-aged man trying to make us into confidants for his relationship to the King.

"And we had the Moorish kiosk nearby when we

wanted to wear Arab, and then we had Hundig's hut, from the first act of *Die Walküre*, when we wanted to wear bearskins and that sort of thing. People said it was a rich man's retreat, and that's what it was. They didn't mind too much. But then there was Herrenchiemsee."

"Also in the French style," Holmes interjected.

"Oh, very French. Linderhof was just modelled on the out-buildings at Versailles, but Herrenchiemsee has that long mansard front—it's a replica of the palace itself. It's enormous. Built on an island in the midst of the Chiemsee. It's very difficult to build something that large on an island you know. Thousands of workmen laboured all day and by torches at night. The silk factories at Lyons worked endlessly. We had three hundred women sewing for seven years just to embroider the cushions. It was vast, and so, naturally, it was very expensive. People said it was the idea of a madman."

"I must say that he sounds mad to me," I said.

"Well, and then he didn't like Herrenchiemsee after it was finished. In one room he had seven portraits of *Le Roi Soleil*, and eight portraits of him in another room. But it didn't seem like Versailles. Ludwig liked to dress up like Louis xiv, and we dined with Louis's bust set up at the table. But there just weren't enough people at Herren-chiemsee to make it seem really French. They're terribly gregarious, you know. Once we had an imaginary ball in the *Galerie des Glaces*. We burned up three thousand wax candles, but when you looked in the mirrors, only myself and the King glided past. And the hairdresser, we had to have him."

"Please, Herr Hornig," Holmes interrupted. "Dr. Watson and I have heard enough of scenes from your past. You said that you had work for me to do. Pray tell me what it is."

"The King is in danger," Hornig said tersely. "He is in danger of losing his crown to his uncle Luitpold, and he is possibly in danger of being incarcerated as a madman for the rest of his life, like his brother Otto."

"I can scarcely make the highly substantial evidence of his past whims disappear," Holmes said. "What role did you wish me to play? Not that I will necessarily undertake to save someone who has devoted twenty years to extravagance and misuse of his revenues."

"The King has very unwisely written a series of letters to the Orléans government of France. Ludwig wishes to borrow money. In exchange for the loan, he offers Bavaria's neutrality in the event of another Franco-Prussian war. Naturally, Bismarck would be most displeased to hear what they contain."

Holmes and I exchanged glances. These were stakes, indeed.

"These letters have been drawn up, but they have not been delivered. It is very dangerous for the French to receive them, but it would be even worse if they should fall into the hands of Uncle Luitpold. The King might be declared unfit to rule.

"I will not dissemble—my allegiance is to the King rather than to the country. I wish to hire you to safeguard the delivery of the letters to France. Second, I want to hire you to assist me in overseeing the fate of the King, and, if it appears that Uncle Luitpold is about to move against him, we must spirit the King across the border. If the letters have gone to France, we'll take him to France; if he should change his mind and not wish to send the letters to France—but if Luitpold finds some other pretext for incarcerating him—then we will take him to Prussia. He has befriended Bismarck in the past, and he would be safe there. And if Bismarck is too annoyed with us, we shall go to Austria."

Holmes sat silently in his chair for a few moments. Yet when he spoke, I heard in his tone the dry note of boredom which had been there since spring.

"You must understand, Herr Hornig, that I am a consulting detective. I take only those cases which interest me. I see no reason to concern myself with the fate of Ludwig. Besides, I have lately been to Munich, and I have no wish to return."

Yes, Holmes had been lately to Munich—in early May for a fortnight. After he returned, he had become particularly dispirited and his use of cocaine had escalated. Nonetheless, perhaps any kind of travel would invigorate him. I hastily said, "But *I* find these Bavarian castles most remarkable."

Holmes sighed.

"You could certainly see the castles," Hornig added. "I know all the secret places, too."

"Why is Ludwig negotiating so recklessly for loans?" Holmes asked.

At this, Hornig drew some large architectural drawings from his leather case. "He wants to build again." Hornig unrolled a drawing of an extremely gothic structure perched on top of a mountain. "It's to be called Falkenstein," Hornig explained. "Rather like Neuschwanstein, but higher, bigger, and more fantastic."

"You ask me to assist in keeping someone on the throne

for the sake of erecting this sort of thing?" Holmes demanded.

Then Hornig unrolled another sheet of paper covered with a blue-ink sketch. "This is the Chinese Palace," Hornig said. Next with a flourish, Hornig unrolled the drawing of a vast Byzantine Palace.

Holmes began to laugh. "What imagination," he cackled. He had not laughed in weeks and the sound was alarming. "But no intelligence."

"If I were back in his favour, I could probably prevent Falkenstein. I don't like heights, do you?"

"So my third service would doubtlessly be to assist you in gaining His Majesty's favour?" Holmes asked. Holmes really cared very little for collecting all the admiration due him, but it was quite apparent that Hornig wanted to claim whatever we accomplished as his own deed.

"Do you know Inspector Lestrade?" I could not help asking.

"Yes, I do," he said. "He was kind enough to give me your name, Mr. Holmes."

"Speaking of Lestrade," Holmes said, "unless I am very much mistaken that is his voice in the vestibule at this very moment."

When Lestrade entered he said, "Still here, Hornig? I thought to have missed you. I really need a word or two with Mr. Holmes alone, if you don't mind."

After giving us the address of his London residence, Hornig left the three of us alone.

"Sordid business, isn't it?" Lestrade said.

"I understand that you referred him to me," Holmes replied.

"Yes, I did. This is big, Holmes. Very big. People in the Cabinet hope you'll look into it."

"Exactly what do you mean?"

"It's to England's advantage, Mr. Holmes, to keep Europe as fractured as possible. If France did give Ludwig a very large loan, it would be quite a blow to Bismarck and to German unification. Prussia is powerful, but she needs Bavaria. No friendly Bavaria and the whole idea of imperial Germany goes unstable. We'd like that, Holmes."

"We?"

"Certain of *them*. Upstairs."

"I dislike assisting a foreign prince whose conduct for twenty years has been unspeakable."

"Things seem to have calmed down about the parties," Lestrade said. "We hear he's lonely. Really rather secluded—just one or two friends at a time. Almost a forlorn figure. Hornig's replacement is a sergeant-major named Hesselschwerdt. For talent, he's got the Hungarian actor Joseph Kainz around, and also the violinist Victor Sigerson."

"Sigerson!" Holmes thundered.

"Yes," Lestrade said, eyeing Holmes curiously.

I saw Holmes calm himself with an effort. With a show of nonchalance, he told Lestrade that since *I* was in the travelling mood, and since certain parties in the Cabinet wished it, he would go to Bavaria.

After Lestrade left, Holmes said to me, "I fear our friend Victor Sigerson is in grave difficulties if Ludwig II has taken a fancy to him."

"I understand that musicians are very much in Ludwig's line," I said.

"I don't pretend to have the keys to Sigerson's heart," Holmes said, "but he is not a degenerate. We will pack for the Dover Express, at once."

❦ 2 ❦

A TEA PARTY
AT LINDERHOF

THE WOODED DOMAIN of Linderhof lies in the swan
country of Bavaria, not far from Oberammergau. As we
journeyed through this country—first by train and then by
carriage and finally on foot—it was obvious why it was called
the swan country, for on every lake floated these majestic
birds. As in England, only royalty can own a swan, and no
one would think of shooting one. The woods were full of
game, though, and as we walked through the forest, we could
hear the wings of birds whirring through the leaves. Along
with Sherlock Holmes and myself was Hornig, an invaluable
guide since he knew all the pathways across the rather wild
and remote landscape, where everything tilted at an angle.

Soon we stepped out of the woods onto a garden path.
Wide avenues lined with hedges cut in fantastic shapes—
mostly swans and peacocks—surrounded the palace.

The exterior of Linderhof was quite gay, in the florid
rococo manner. A pediment of elaborately carved figures
decorated the front, but my eye was captivated by a golden

coach with six plumed horses, gleaming white, that stood at the door.

"Are we not in danger of meeting Ludwig?" Holmes asked. "It would appear he is about to make a journey."

"Oh, no," Hornig replied, "the coach is always ready."

Just as though he were the master of the place, Hornig ran boldly up the stairs and into the front door, which stood carelessly open. Holmes and I followed Hornig into the vestibule dominated by a large equestrian statue of Louis XIV. The walls were covered with fleur-de-lis. All the furnishings were exceedingly rich—velvet, bronze, and marble. We heard footsteps approaching. Hornig was not at all frightened when a tall, thin blond man entered. Nor did the fellow seem surprised to see Hornig, who introduced the newcomer as Alphonse Welcker. "This is Mr. Holmes, who will assist us in looking out for the King's interests," he explained, "and Dr. Watson, his constant companion."

"We may have need of a doctor," Welcker said.

"You see, Alphonse, like myself," Hornig explained, "has the King's health in mind."

"Tell me," Holmes asked Welcker, "is the violinist Sigerson about?"

Welcker exchanged glances with Hornig. "Sigerson is not exactly one of us," Welcker said. "I don't know if he can be trusted. Do you like him?"

"I should be very much displeased if anything were to inconvenience Sigerson," Holmes responded.

"Oh, you *do* like him," Welcker said. "Well, he's not too happy here. He wants to go to Munich and give violin lessons. He's one of those who likes children, you know what I mean."

"I'm certain that you misconstrue Sigerson's character," Holmes said. "Dr. Watson and I can both vouch for him."

Actually I had always thought Sigerson to be an odd fellow, and I didn't particularly like him. But if Sigerson's safety concerned Holmes, I was glad of it, for certainly Holmes's interest was a much more healthy mental state than the melancholia he had experienced lately during much of the spring.

"Well, the King keeps his musician around like a bear on a string. I hope Sigerson doesn't think he's going to replace me," Welcker said petulantly.

"I haven't the slightest doubt that the very idea is the substance of his nightmares," Holmes said.

"Where are they now?" Hornig asked.

"They and the Sergeant-Major are at the kiosk. I'll take you," Welcker replied.

Soon we were peering through the leaves of the potted orange trees at the kiosk. At a table, on which were cups of coffee—we could smell the Turkish aroma of the coffee and of the smoke from long pipes—sat three figures, the most splendid of which appeared to be King Louis XIV.

"That's Ludwig," Hornig explained.

Also at the table was a bust of Marie Antoinette. Ludwig was holding a cup of coffee to her lips as though the statue would shortly begin to sip it.

"*La sainte-reine*," Ludwig mumbled, "here's to your health. And long life. May it be filled with sadness. Exquisite sorrow."

His words evaporated in the volume of the vast outdoors. An immense sky vaulted the tea table. The mountains around us seemed austere and remote. Never have I heard so lonely a voice, such sad folly.

Ludwig wore a splendid period-costume of golden satin covered with fleur-de-lis. A wig of chestnut curls cascaded over his shoulders and down his back. Beside him sat an obese man in Arabian robes. He was identified as Hesselschwerdt, whom apparently both Hornig and Welcker feared and disliked.

"Just look at his manners," Welcker whispered to Hornig. Hesselschwerdt was taking enormous bites from a huge sausage. The King was eating a dainty, creme-filled pastry.

The third person seated at the table was Victor Sigerson. He wore knee breeches and a little white wig tied back with a black ribbon. "The King wishes him to resemble Mozart," Holmes said in my ear. The expression on Sigerson's face was one of boredom and anxiety. A large pastry, untouched by the golden fork, sat on a china plate in front of him.

"If you're not going to eat that," Ludwig said, "Marie would probably like it."

"Very well," Sigerson said, and he pulled up his chair closer to the bust of Marie Antoinette. I wondered if I were losing my wits. Quite solemnly Mozart-Sigerson brought a forkful of cake up to the lips of the statue. After the cake was held before her for a moment, Ludwig opened his mouth, pretended to be absorbed in looking at something else, and Mozart popped the cake into the King's mouth! He chewed and swallowed. This ritual was repeated several times.

"Let her eat bread," Hesselschwerdt said with a cruel laugh.

Ludwig clapped his hands and a servant appeared. He was swaddled in white Arabian robes, but he also wore a strange white mask that entirely covered his face, so that no inch of human flesh or hair was visible. When I looked questioningly at Hornig, he explained that this was a servant whom Ludwig had found ugly, and the mask was to keep His Majesty from having to see the displeasing face. Why the servant was not merely replaced I never learned. Presently the servant appeared with a loaf of French bread, which Hesselschwerdt tore into bits and offered to the queen, then ate as an accompaniment to his sausage.

During this astonishing tableau, I had quite forgotten my friend Holmes. Now he placed his hand on my shoulder. His hand was trembling. When I glanced at his face, the veins were standing out on his forehead. I had thought Holmes would have been more amused than angered by this harmless folly, but he was not.

"I fear for Victor's safety," he said.

"Isn't it time," Ludwig asked his friends, "to plan a memorial mass for the queen? I think there should be a little, tiny guillotine on the altar this year." He clapped his hands and again the Arabian-swaddled servant appeared, received an order, and then disappeared down a pathway.

Holmes spoke urgently into Welcker's ear, and then after signifying that Hornig and I were to stay behind, he and Welcker went in pursuit of the servant.

"Hesselschwerdt," the King said, "would you mind doing a little, tiny favour for me?"

"What is it?" Hesselschwerdt replied rudely.

"How dare he address the King like that!" Hornig said in my ear.

"I have letters ready for France, but I really can't trust anybody these days, do you think?"

"Everybody loves Your Majesty," Hesselschwerdt said without conviction.

"What do you think, my handsome Mozart?" the King asked.

"I should counsel discretion," Sigerson answered bitterly. "But why do you ask me for advice? I'm nothing but a mediocre musician whose pupils need him in Munich."

"Well, if you're going to Munich," Ludwig said to Sigerson, "would you mind taking—"

"Wait!" Hesselschwerdt interrupted. "You were about to ask me to do a little, tiny favour, and now, right in front of me, you're about to ask him to do it! I'm shocked and hurt."

"I shall be glad to take your letters to Munich," Sigerson said. He removed the Mozartian wig and placed it on the table.

"See what a nice man he is," Ludwig taunted Hesselschwerdt.

"He just wants to slip away," the Sergeant-Major said.

"Hmmm. Perhaps you're right. Well, would *you* then, my valiant soldier, my courier, my Hesselschwerdt, take charge of these letters?"

He handled a small bundle of envelopes to Hesselschwerdt. They were tied with a purple velvet ribbon.

"I'm very glad you decided to do this," Hesselschwerdt said. "And it serves Bismarck right. He could have given us a loan—you asked him first."

"I've asked nearly everyone," the King said sadly, "the

Shah of Persia, the Rothschilds, the Erlangers."

At this moment the servant reappeared. Actually, I heard the servant before I saw him. He was humming loudly a tune I happened to recognize—"Tales from the Vienna Woods."

Sigerson jumped and looked up sharply. After the servant had attended to Ludwig, he went away humming some other tune that I didn't recognize.

"You know," Sigerson said, "I should like to take a stroll, if you don't mind."

"If you try to run away," Ludwig said, "I'll have one of your fingers cut off."

I gasped involuntarily. Everything had seemed so light-hearted as they had had their mad tea in the sunshine. And yet, here was a threat of the most callous sort, spoken with no trace of gaiety.

"And I should like to go straight to Munich," said Hesselschwerdt, getting up from the table.

"I'll be left alone," Ludwig complained. "Sigerson, go get your violin and play for me. You can walk later."

Hornig and I crouched low among the citrus trees for a while, but once Sigerson commenced playing we were able to slip away to meet Holmes and Welcker deep in the garden. Holmes was just stepping out of the Arabian clothing.

"Holmes!" I said. "Was that you?"

"Yes, Watson. Did anything of interest happen before I appeared on the scene?"

I told Holmes that Hesselschwerdt had been given the packet of incriminating letters.

"Is Hesselschwerdt to be trusted?" Holmes said.

Hornig and Welcker exchanged a glance and then said with one voice, "No."

"Please follow him, Herr Holmes," Hornig added.

"I cannot," Holmes said. "I have another appointment."

"No," Hornig said earnestly. "You cannot. This is the reason that I engaged your services."

"I must speak to Dr. Watson for a moment, alone," Holmes said.

We withdrew to the other side of a noisy fountain. "Watson, I shall have to ask you to follow Hesselschwerdt. I've arranged to meet Sigerson, and I must not miss the appointment."

"Arranged to meet Sigerson? How?"

"By humming. First I informed him of my presence by humming a tune that he has heard me perform rather poorly, I'm afraid, on the violin."

"I noticed the Arabian servant was humming 'Tales from the Vienna Woods,'" I said. "But after that, I didn't see you pass him a note."

"That's because I did not pass a note. One of Ludwig's toys is a replica of Hundig's hut. By humming Hundig's music I told Sigerson to meet me there, as soon as possible."

"Wonderful," I said.

"I don't wish Hornig and Welcker to know, obviously."

So Holmes and I returned to them, and Holmes explained firmly that it was Hornig and I who would have to pursue the Sergeant-Major. Holmes scarcely gave us instructions as to what to do. He seemed extremely concerned about Sigerson.

Welcker was easily able to obtain horses and a carriage for us from the Linderhof stables, and soon Hornig and I were heading for Munich in pursuit of Sergeant-Major

Hesselschwerdt. As it turned out, we would go together only as far as Oberammergau, where an unforeseen event would make us part company.

Hornig, who was most displeased that Holmes was not with us, insisted on talking the whole way. His swarthy countenance was a mobile one, but his features merely slid from one unpleasant expression to another. At one point he had the audacity to suggest that Sigerson was about to replace me in Holmes's affection. "I can read the signs about this sort of thing," he bragged.

I told him that I would not hear another word of such vile insinuations about Holmes's regard for Sigerson. Much less about myself. Holmes had always taken a special interest in the careers of certain musicians. "Just like Ludwig," Hornig sneered.

When we reached Oberammergau, we saw that Hesselschwerdt's carriage had stopped outside a tavern, so we stopped also. Being unknown to Hesselschwerdt, I went into the tavern to observe his activities there. I saw him meet two other gentlemen to whom he immediately handed the correspondence.

One of the newcomers, obviously a man of rank, was called Count Holnstein. The other was a powerfully built physician, a Dr. Gudden. When I saw Hesselschwerdt hand Ludwig's letters over to these two, I decided to report at once to Hornig.

Although clearly distressed, Hornig bore my description of Count Holnstein with equanimity. But when I mentioned the physician, he exclaimed, "Dr. Gudden is the head of the Asylum for the Insane in Munich!" Shouting that he must save the King, he ran recklessly into the tavern before I could stop him. I stood at the door, helplessly watching him attempt to wrest the letters from the hands of Count Holnstein. The Count called for his attendants, and in very short order it was evident that Hornig was under arrest. I determined to slip away and return with news of these developments to Holmes. Though it was not my habit to question the tactics of Sherlock Holmes, I could not help but wonder if his rendezvous with Sigerson at Hundig's hut had been a wise move.

It was late afternoon when I arrived at Linderhof and found my way to Hundig's hut. I approached the hut from the rear, and thus I was able to look in at a small window. There sat Holmes, squarely in front of the door with his back to me. His long legs were crossed before him, and his hands were clasped behind his head. I was just about to make my presence known by tapping on the glass when the front door burst open and Victor Sigerson ran in. "I'm a captive here," he shrieked, his voice an octave higher than normal. To my total astonishment, he flung himself into Holmes's arms and sobbed like a woman. "I'm so frightened I don't dare sleep." Like a mother, Holmes held and comforted him. I was so amazed that I turned my eyes away from the scene.

Feeling like an intruder, I withdrew a bit from the hut. I confess that I felt extremely confused by what I had witnessed. The man was sobbing in Holmes's arms!

It was a good thing I had posted myself away from the scene, because I soon noted that Ludwig and Welcker, both dressed in bearskins, were making their way toward the hut. They were accompanied by four or five servants who were carrying drinking horns, large bowls of fruit, and a suckling pig. Quickly I ran into the hut. Holmes and Sigerson were seated across a rude table from each other, apparently deep in earnest conversation. I merely said, "Ludwig is coming," and they both quickly got up.

"The violin must not be left behind," Sigerson said.

While Sigerson hurried out of the door and down the path in the direction of the palace, Holmes and I concealed ourselves in an adjacent wooded area. Once we were safe, I reported that Hornig and the letters had been captured.

"The matter is most serious, then," Holmes said. "It would appear that a move against Ludwig is imminent."

I agreed, and then remained silent.

"Not a pleasant trip for you?" Holmes asked. His keen habit of observation revealed that I was in a state of some confusion.

"It's a strange country," I said.

"Yes, you have the expression of one who has seen something quite unexpected, even shocking."

I scarcely knew how to broach the subject. "I am amazed to note that Sigerson has been crying," I said.

"Then, my dear Watson, I must explain something to you. The person whom you saw was not Victor Sigerson, but his twin sister."

I gasped, "The resemblance is most remarkable."

"Victor has lent her his clothes, as you saw."

"Shouldn't she be sent home?"

"Indeed she should. And I have just done that." He went on, "It would be impossible to rescue them both, and so we shall be content with taking Victor back to London with us."

"Back to London!" I said. But I thought, why not dispatch Sigerson with the girl?

"Sigerson sent word by his twin sister that he is quite willing to go." Holmes began to pace about on the forest floor.

"Should we not warn Ludwig that his letters have been intercepted?"

Holmes agreed that we should, but, it seemed to me, rather reluctantly. Never before had I seen him engaged for a purpose and then show so little interest in drawing it to a satisfactory conclusion! He expressed great concern for the fate of Victor Sigerson, very little for King Ludwig II of Bavaria.

I said as much.

"You saw the King, just as I did," Holmes responded sadly. "What is your clinical opinion of him?"

"He is insane," I said. The tableau of three grown men playing tea-party like a trio of little girls rose again in my mind, and it seemed more sinister as a recollection than it had when I first witnessed it.

"I do not think that the insane should rule," Holmes said. "I believe George III of England used to mistake a certain copper beech in Windsor Park for the King of Prussia, but at least we British surrounded our less competent kings with able ministers. Look at Ludwig's advisors. His hairdresser obviously has the power of a cabinet minister."

"Is there nothing we can do for him?"

"What would you suggest?" Holmes asked.

I had no reply.

Nonetheless, we crouched in the forest of Linderhof,

not far from Hundig's hut, and waited for the feast to end. We saw the King, dressed in a brown bearskin fastened with claws over the shoulder, come out of the hut to step back into the bushes several times during the revelry.

At length, Welcker emerged from the hut alone, and we seized those few moments to tell him what had befallen his friend Hornig. But Welcker was too drunk from mead to understand what was being said to him. "Hornig has been arrested by Count Holnstein. Dr. Gudden is prepared to take the King to the Munich Asylum!" Holmes repeated, and he shook the man.

"No," Welcker said. He seemed to steady himself. "No, next the King and I go to Neuschwanstein."

"Then you had better go," Holmes snapped.

❊ 3 ❊

A MOUNTAIN CHASE

AFTER DELIVERING THE warning, Holmes and I
went back to the kiosk, where he had arranged to meet
Sigerson at midnight. Holmes seemed in quite a state of
excitement. He started several topics of conversation,
but abandoned each of them. The marriage of John
Stuart Mill and his wife Harriet seemed to fascinate him.
"A thoroughly productive team," Holmes said. "They
were as congenial as though they were brother and
sister." I had the impression that there was something
Holmes particularly wished to discuss, but each time he
seemed close to settling on a topic he changed it to
something else.

Thus, we passed the long night in conversation while
we waited for Sigerson. The nearly full moon appeared in
one corner of the window, crossed the window, and passed
out of sight. At one point, we heard the sound of horses'
hooves, and Holmes made an excursion to investigate.
When he returned to the pavilion, he said that he had seen

the King, Welcker, and the swaddled servant get in the royal coach.

"Odd time of day for travel," I observed.

Holmes reminded me that Ludwig was especially fond of night rides through the mountains. "Sometimes he stops at a peasant's hovel and leaves the family a pot of lilies."

"Did he fill the carriage with lilies?"

"No, but the servant was carrying the bust of Marie Antoinette."

Holmes seemed to be musing on something, and at last he said, "I keep thinking that it was peculiar that the servant was carrying the bust upside down. Does that suggest anything to you, Watson?"

"Upside down?"

Holmes leapt to his feet. "A distress signal! Come, Watson," he commanded. "We must go to the palace."

"But Sigerson may come at any moment," I protested.

"I fear," Holmes said grimly, "that he has already left." As we rushed toward the palace, Holmes cursed himself for having suggested the disguise by assuming it himself, with Welcker's aid, at the tea party—a disguise that had now been used to kidnap Sigerson.

The full moon illuminated the rococo decorations on the castle façade. Our long shadows stole after us as we crossed the drive. I thought I heard footsteps behind us, but, glancing back, I saw only the kiosk, like a fairy structure half-hidden by the night. Holmes charged straight to the front door and tried it. This time the door was locked. As Holmes began to fit his wire into the lock, we both became aware of a figure standing below us at the edge of the steps. He shone his torch upon us, and we were pinioned in a circle of light before the palace door.

The figure holding the light said, "Mr. Holmes?"

Holmes began slowly to descend the steps, and the man withdrew the light from our eyes and beamed it on the pavement. He was humbly dressed.

"I believe you are the groom," Holmes said. "Oster-holzer?"

"Yes, sir. Welcker has left me with a message for you."

"Pray let us hear it," Holmes said icily.

"They've taken the violinist with them to Neuschwan-stein. Welcker thought you . . . well, that you wouldn't help the King if they didn't take him along."

"And?"

"I've got a carriage all ready, and we can follow them up the mountain, if you're willing, sir."

"I would be much obliged if we could start at once," Holmes said. "I assume you are very familiar with the road?"

"Oh, yes, sir. First we will pass Hohenschwangau, the little palace, and then Neuschwanstein is a mile on and higher in the mountains."

The groom took the driver's seat, and soon we were rattling over the mountain road on the trail of the royal carriage. Fortunately the moon was bright and illumined the road. But the woods on both sides were black enough to have concealed an army, if one had been hidden there.

Holmes spoke urgently to Osterholzer, "Don't spare the horses! We must come as close to the royal coach as possible."

Osterholzer replied, "Then we shall have to stop at

Hohenschwangau to change the horses." The whip cracked in the air as the groom urged the horses on.

Osterholzer appeared to be the most normal and likable of any member of the King's entourage whom we had encountered. He was full of respect for Holmes, and it was clear he had some genuine and simple love of the King as his sovereign. "Fine fellow," I remarked to Holmes.

Holmes replied that it was his impression in general that the mountain folk were loyal to the King. "Their King is a dreamer," he continued, "and they would certainly prefer to build for him than to fight for the Prussian war machine. If he were well enough to use that reservoir of loyalty, his uncle would have a very difficult time in unseating him."

The other carriage had perhaps an hour's start on us, but one time as we were descending a curving road, I thought that I caught a glimpse of ivory and gold rushing along a road through the valley far below.

At length, the lights of Hohenschwangau Palace emerged from the darkness. We determined we must indeed take on fresh horses, though the King's party had gone on to Neuschwanstein. Osterholzer had been so unsparing of ours, at Holmes's insistence, that we all feared they would drop in the traces. As we pulled into the barn, I recognized the insignia emblazoned on another coach. This party had arrived shortly before us—it was now three in the morning—and the grooms were still tending their horses. There were several carriages in that party; the one that I recognized bore the insignia of Count Holnstein.

I quickly communicated my observation to Holmes and to Osterholzer. After questioning the other grooms, whom he knew well, Osterholzer learned that not only Count Holnstein but also Dr. Gudden had arrived, and that they had thought the King was to be found at Hohenschwangau. The King's valet, who had been working more for Sergeant-Major Hesselschwerdt than for His Majesty, had betrayed Ludwig's plans to leave Linderhof.

Holmes and Osterholzer agreed that the latter should stay behind to try to learn more of the conspirators' plans, while Holmes and I would rush on, with fresh horses, to Neuschwanstein. Soon Holmes and I were up on the driver's box, and Holmes was applying the whip more liberally than ever the groom had done. Although we had lost time by the stop, our horses were fresher than the King's and with the very steep terrain before us, it was possible that we might overtake them. Our four black steeds were all muscle and spirit, and they ran like the possessed. The horses were so dark they seemed like bits of the night.

It was Holmes's intention to remove Sigerson from the King's power and then to do what he could to help the King escape to the Austrian Tyrol, which was only an hour's drive. The rushing wind and jolting caused by our terrible pace made it difficult to talk on the box, but I could not help remarking to Holmes that he seemed to have taken pity on the King at last.

"He is surrounded by traitors and a powerful net is closing around him," Holmes replied. "His friends have no experience that would be of service to him now, no matter how loyal they may be. If I had a dozen fellows as stout-hearted as the groom, I would feel more confident of victory, but we must do what we can."

The road was very winding, and many times I felt my heart in my throat as we swung around a turn. Sometimes the full moon was shrouded with clouds, but occasionally it revealed chasms of stupefying steepness which yawned, it seemed, at the very edge of our way. Sometimes sparks flew from the shoes of the horses on the rocky road.

Holmes was eager to overtake the royal carriage before it reached Neuschwanstein, wanting to catch the King in isolation and then drive straight on to the Tyrol. He feared that once the King reached the castle, he would regard it as a safer place than the open road and refuse to go on.

Yet, fly as we did, we seemed unable to gain on the royal coach. Holmes lashed the horses without mercy, and the sweat from their haunches stung our faces. At last the battlements of Neuschwanstein rose above us, white and gleaming in the moonlight. It was a sight of breathtaking beauty. Towers, turrets, and pinnacles all thrust upward. It seemed that humans could never have constructed so steep a castle at such a lofty height.

"It is difficult to believe that a soul capable of that is beyond cure," I said. I was so jounced by our speed that I could scarcely speak.

At that moment we saw the royal coach—all ivory and gold, pulled by the white horses—perhaps a mile of winding road below the entrance to the castle, but only half a mile above us. Unfortunately they saw us too, and apparently surmised that we were in pursuit. I clearly saw the coachman raise his glittering whip in the moonlight and lash out at the horses. Alas, there was no way we could communicate we were in friendly pursuit.

Holmes redoubled his efforts, and we began to close on the very tired horses of the King. But what magnificent animals they were! Though our black horses were fresh, we had but four of them. The King's carriage was pulled by six horses, each apparently selected for its ability to race up mountain roads. Nonetheless we were gradually closing in on them.

I had just yelled, "We'll catch them," when with horror I saw a huge boulder in the King's path. Immediately Ludwig's coach swung around the boulder and seemed to lunge toward the abyss. For a moment his carriage teetered on the brink of the chasm, but then the six strong horses all courageously pulled together and drew the coach from the void. In an instant they were coursing forward again, and we were swinging around the boulder in the road. I felt the wheels on one side leave the roadbed, and then all that I recall was Holmes's voice shouting, "Jump, Watson! Jump!"

4

DISASTER AT NEUSCHWANSTEIN

When I regained consciousness, it was dawn. The first thing I saw was the rosy light bathing the swan-castle. I realized that my body was lodged against a sturdy pine tree, and that this tree had saved my life. Far below I could see the mangled carcasses of the horses and the splintered carriage.

Carefully, I tried to move my body. It was so painful an effort that I almost lost consciousness again. Yet even then I thought I had no bones broken, though my body had been battered into a mass of bruises. I was merely cold and stiff from having lain on the slope in the night hours.

I looked around for Holmes. Perhaps he, too, had been saved by some tree or shrub, or perhaps he had leapt onto the road. I knew that if he were alive and conscious he was now looking for me.

I began to hear strange noises, as though a troop were on the road below. I tried to discern what might be occurring. Although the morning light struck the ramparts of the castle, it was still quite grey at lesser heights. I listened intently to the sounds of men on the move. Presently I saw a troop of peasants carrying torches and rushing up the mountain. They were armed with scythes, poles, axes, and even a few rifles. On their tunics, several of them had painted crude outlines of lilies or of swans.

At the time I could not account for this phenomenon, but later I learned that the honest Osterholzer had organized the stableboys and their relatives in the village to climb the mountain in order to protect the King from his Uncle Luitpold's emissaries. When they reached the portion of road directly below me, I tried to raise myself to signal to them, but I could not. The effort was too much for me, and again I slipped into unconsciousness against the pine.

I think it must have been the morning sun that finally warmed and woke me. I felt stronger, and by slow and painful degrees I was able to stand up. I glanced everywhere for some sign of Holmes, but there was none. When I gained the road, I saw by the multitudinous footprints that the peasant army had tramped by. It seemed to me best to try to reach the castle, and so I began to follow in their footsteps.

Before I had gone five yards, I saw a familiar object beside the road. It was Holmes's deerstalker cap. The brush had been smashed by the passage of his body, and it seemed fairly certain to me that he, too, had been caught against the trunk of a tree. At least I saw no sign of any further descent. Then I noticed another garment. It was a lavender scarf such as I had seen tied around the throat of Welcker.

These discoveries gave me cause for rejoicing, for I felt secure in deducing that after our carriage had gone over the edge, Ludwig—good king—had ordered his to stop and sent Welcker to investigate. Perhaps Holmes had already been conveyed to the castle where he was receiving medical treatment.

The last fifty yards to Neuschwanstein Castle were on a stone road atop a high, buttressed foundation. As I limped toward the castle portal, that fantastic building loomed ever-larger above me. The tops of the walls were crenellated, and flags danced atop the pinnacles of the turrets. The whole medieval display made me feel I was entering a dream landscape.

Or *trying* to enter it, for I stood at the gate and banged for several minutes without anyone taking notice. As I stood there and waited, a swan rose up from the waters lying in the chasm near the castle. Its snowy wings flashing in the morning sun, the bird flew over the wooded mountains. I watched until it was a speck in the sky, and then I commenced pounding on the gate again.

At last I gained entry and asked to see either Welcker or Osterholzer. The area was filled with peasants who stood in small groups, discussing what actions they might take if anyone tried to depose their King. One of them with a swan painted on his chest said that he would fight for Ludwig.

Welcker was glad to see me.

"My dear fellow, we had no idea you were in the carriage, too. We have need of your professional services," he said.

"Holmes?" I asked.

"He lies unconscious in the infirmary." As we hurried through the corridors, Welcker also expressed the hope that

I might be able to persuade the King to escape into the Tyrol.

"Yes," I said. I could only confirm the danger: "Count Holnstein will surely be here soon."

"Unfortunately, His Majesty thinks that he might be arrested more easily on the road. Here the peasants protect him."

"What have you done for Holmes?" I asked.

"We didn't know what to do." He paused. "Tell me, Dr. Watson, what steps do you think Ludwig should take, if he refuses to flee?"

"Has he planned any counter-measures against Munich?" The corridors of the palace seemed endless.

"He sent for Count Dürckheim, his only friend among the nobility, and he has decided to have Count Holnstein arrested."

Holmes lay on a narrow bed carefully tucked round with white sheets. He was pale as death, but he breathed slightly. I took his pulse, which was strong, and rolled back the lid of his eye. He had suffered a trauma to the head. The area around his temple was bruised and inflamed. I spoke to him and shook him, but there was no sign of consciousness.

In such cases there is very little medical science can offer. One must wait for the brain to heal itself and for the patient to regain consciousness. Welcker had stationed a blond German girl, Ilse, who seemed to be a competent nurse. She said that she rubbed Holmes's arms and legs from time to time to promote circulation. After asking her a few questions about her patient, I concluded she had done as much as anyone could. I proposed to Welcker that I simply remain in the infirmary.

Welcker thought that I would do well to rest, but he

added, "I hope that you will be willing to confer with His Majesty, Count Dürckheim, and myself about our course of action."

I looked at the immobile face of Holmes. "I wish that he might attend this conference," I replied and passed my hand over Holmes's forehead.

Then it occurred to me to ask about Sigerson, who had not been mentioned.

"Sigerson is not well," Welcker answered evasively.

"How so?" I asked. "Is he not here?"

"Yes," Welcker said. "But, to be exact, he is in the dungeon."

"The dungeon?"

"When I brought Herr Holmes into our carriage, after your mishap on the road, Sigerson became excessively disturbed. His Majesty was very displeased. Sigerson accused us of having killed Holmes, but, of course, we were attempting to save him. With the exception of His Majesty, I have scarcely ever seen a man so volatile as Sigerson."

"And so Ludwig incarcerated him?"

Welcker nodded.

After I sent Ilse and Welcker away, I lay down on the small bed across from the one occupied by Holmes. I had meant to stay awake to watch him, but, being entirely exhausted, I soon began to doze.

I was awakened by someone pulling at my sleeve and then shaking my hand. To my astonishment, it was Sigerson. He was pale and wan in appearance but certainly reasonable.

"How is your patient?" he asked with an expression of genuine concern.

I told him what I could of Holmes's condition, and that I hoped he would awaken naturally in a few hours.

"I see they have released you," I said.

"No. I released myself. I'm rather good with locks, you know. These are mere toys, stage scenery rather than a real dungeon, though I suppose they would hold anyone who was not an expert."

When I asked Sigerson what he planned to do next, he said that he intended to return to the dungeon.

"I'm safer there," he added.

"Safer from whom?"

"His Majesty. He has developed an attraction toward me." Sigerson blushed as he uttered these words.

"Then back to the dungeon, by all means," I said, after carefully listening to his description of the dungeon's location in the castle.

He reached out his fingers as if to touch Holmes, but hesitated. "It's a terrible bruise on his head," he said apprehensively.

I explained that there is such a plentiful blood supply to the head that bruises often appear more dramatic than dangerous.

Sigerson glanced at me anxiously. "Yet he has been unconscious for some hours. Suppose he should simply never wake up?"

Of course the idea had occurred to me as well, but I did not want to reinforce Sigerson's distress. "At least," I said, "he is not in pain."

We stood and watched Holmes continue his shallow breathing for some moments. Suddenly Sigerson reached forward and squeezed the back of Holmes's hand. He glanced at me and said softly, "The very instant there is any change you shall contrive to send me word."

It was a command as much as a request. I murmured, "Of course."

At that moment we heard the tramp of feet on the stone road leading to the castle. When we passed through the French doors onto a small balcony, we saw a mixed group of peasants and city-dressed men. The peasants had arrested Count Holnstein and the Munich Commission. Apparently having been forced to march on foot up the mountain from Hohenschwangau to Neuschwanstein, the noblemen were dusty, disarrayed, and weary.

We watched them file into the courtyard, and then Ludwig himself appeared at a high window. It was the first time I had seen him appear as other than Louis XIV.

He was imperial. His voice—as booming as an orator's—rang out over the heads of his enemies. He had the large barrel chest and the girth of a baritone. I could not understand every word of his German address, but Sigerson translated for me. Ludwig promised to throw the rebels into the dungeon and then to behead them. He was particularly angry with Count Holnstein, who was a distant relative. He reminded Holnstein of how, sixteen years before, he had been a trusted courier between Ludwig and Bismarck, how he had brought Bismarck's letter proposing a plan for German unification, and so forth. Sigerson turned from the window with a sigh.

"Now he has lapsed into believing he is Parsifal. Their crime is that they have violated the Castle of the Holy Grail. He is avowing the Holy Grail itself is here in the castle's throne room. Since he wants to throw them all in the dungeon, I had better put myself there."

In a few hours, I looked out the window and was amazed to see the Commissioners being brought out of the dungeon and placed in a carriage. *Why, Ludwig?* I thought as they were driven away. *You had the upper hand.*

I turned from the spectacle to massage Holmes's chest and limbs. I thought his facial colour was somewhat better, and his eyelids quivered as though he were making an effort to awaken. At length, however, his breathing became deeper, and he seemed to settle into a more normal sleep.

Pressure on the brain could be relieved by an operation. I looked at my hands. The *Lancet* had carried an article on a new technique—a scraping away of the blood clot. My stubby fingers looked awkward and incompetent. My hands began to tremble.

❧ 5 ❧

ROYAL MUSIC

FRIDAY, JUNE 11, 1886, was a misty, gloomy day, and Ilse told me we were sure to have a storm that night. I stayed in the infirmary all morning, assisting her in changing the bed linens. When Ilse was out of the room, I talked to Holmes and reminded him that he must try to get well. There was no visible response, but I could not help but hope that something in his dreaming mind was hearing me.

I felt again that the King's situation was hopeless, and it occurred to me that it would be to Sigerson's benefit to leave at once. I determined to visit him in his cell and tell him so.

When I found Sigerson, he was gnawing on a chicken leg. He said that it was a good thing that he could get in and out, as no one had brought him anything to eat. He had found food on his own.

"I am surprised Welcker has not had something sent to you," I said.

Sigerson laughed at the suggestion. "Welcker sees me as a rival for the King's affection."

Seating myself on one of the hard bunks in the cell, I asked, "Do you not think it wise for you to leave the castle?"

"I'll keep well enough here."

"The King's attraction?"

Sigerson stalked to one end of the cell and turned dramatically. "What sort of man do you take me for, Dr. Watson? Do you think that I would abandon you and Holmes?"

I really had no idea what advantage he thought his presence lent to our situation. "Well," I said. "How will you spend the morning?"

"I have retrieved my violin from the luggage. I will spend the morning practicing."

As I left the dungeon, I heard him practicing scales.

After lunch, Welcker appeared in the infirmary and announced, "His Majesty wishes you to come for an audience."

First I checked Holmes's condition, and then I accompanied Welcker through long passageways decorated with immense frescoes, each depicting the life of a legendary warrior from German mythology. Everything seemed gloomy and heavy, until we walked into the King's own apartment. Here were paintings of scenes from Wagner's *Tannhäuser*, and the room was vaulted into a high grotto opening onto an adjoining balcony.

The King lurked in a corner of the room for a few moments, but the gentleman at his side, whom I took to be

Count Dürckheim, walked quickly across the room on his short bandy legs to greet me. The little Count cut a rather ridiculous figure, dressed in a very elaborate and expensive coat, but as soon as I bowed in response to his greeting, I noticed his eyes—weary, shrewd, and above all, wise.

He greeted me like a brother and said how good it was of me to come all the way from England to advise His Majesty. He had heard much of my reputation for advising Her Royal Highness Victoria. All of this was preposterous, of course, but I saw that a role had already been designed for me to play, and I tried to accommodate myself to it.

After several moments of effusive greeting by Count Dürckheim, the King warily edged himself out of the corner. When he was within ten yards of me, he suddenly moved more naturally, held out his hand to me, and said simply, "I'm Ludwig."

I bowed and told him that I was at his service.

"You are a neutral observer," he began, "but could you give up your castles, if you were I, and flee to an ugly foreign country—perhaps forever?"

I scarcely knew how to answer this question so as not to lose his confidence immediately.

"May I ask Your Majesty a question?" I said. And when he assented, I asked, "Did I not see Count Holnstein and his party released and placed in their carriages? Why were they released?"

Ludwig began to pull nervously at his collar, which was a small ruff encircling his neck. "I was afraid," he said, "that I would cut off their heads. So I let them go. Once I almost had somebody's hands cut off, a musician who played badly."

I thought of poor Sigerson and shuddered; at least he played well. To the King I said, "What do you think the rebels will do next?"

"They're probably talking with Uncle Luitpold."

"Do you think they will return, in greater numbers?"

The King did not answer. He walked slowly and thoughtfully to a window which was hung with rich velvet curtains embroidered with swans. All at once, Ludwig lifted a curtain and disappeared behind it. His voice came to us muffled from behind the velvet. "I would hide until they left again."

Count Dürckheim strode to the curtain and slowly pulled it aside. "But suppose," the Count said gently, "they were to find you?"

I began to pace briskly about the room and to offer advice: "The people adore Your Majesty. They would not forget him, were he gone for a short time. Perhaps they would even send him money in Austria to build a castle there." The King stepped out from the curtain and shyly approached me. "Yes," I went on, "there is nothing to lose in taking a short trip—it's really almost next door."

The King asked, "Do you know my brother Otto?"

"I have not had the pleasure."

"He was known as 'The Merry Otto.' But one day his brain failed him. He turned into an animal, Dr. Watson."

"Most unfortunate," I commiserated.

"The last time I saw him I simply dissolved in grief."

"And Otto?"

"He smiled and entertained himself with some stuffed toys. I could not bear to leave him." Ludwig was quite overcome in his recollection. "His keepers took him away." He put his head in his hands. "Am I, Dr. Watson, going the way of Otto?"

"In my opinion," I said, "to stay here is madness; to flee is sanity and health and hope for future happiness."

The King did not reply but walked excitedly around the room several times and then out on the balcony. I did not like to see him go out on the open balcony in such a disturbed frame of mind. Count Dürckheim exchanged an uneasy glance with me and then joined the King on the balcony. The little Count was half the size of the over-weight and powerful King, and I doubted that he could restrain the King should he decide to jump.

Ludwig dropped his hand on Dürckheim's shoulder and then stared down into his face. "You," Ludwig said in a puzzled manner, "you . . . I don't want you. Send Dr. Watson here."

Thus I stood quietly in Dürckheim's place beside the King.

"Are you a lover of music?" he asked me.

"Indeed," I replied.

Together we stared out past the castle's turrets and walls to the rugged countryside which was covered with mist and grey clouds. It seemed to be raining in the distance.

"Then hum for me," he said, "the opening music from *Die Walküre.*"

I was struck dumb by the suggestion. I stood quietly beside him and hoped that the idea would evaporate.

He swung his whole body around and scowled into my face. "Hum!" he commanded, his eyes flashing.

"It happens to have slipped my mind," I said.

"When Siegmund and Siegliende come together in Hundig's hut—what is the music doing?"

"Of course my interests lie along the lines of Anglo-Saxon mythology rather than the Teutonic. Now had there been an opera based on Beowulf—"

"Imposter!" shrieked the King. "You are an imposter. You know nothing about music! How can you advise my soul?"

In a terrific rage, he upbraided Dürckheim and Welcker for having engaged my services. He claimed that he had followed their advice exactly and what had it brought him? Ludwig called for his guard, ordered that I be marched off to the dungeon, and then insisted impulsively on accompanying me to prison—he wanted to be sure I would be comfortable there. As we passed servants, he sent them to fetch comforters. Three servants scurried behind us, their arms piled high with satin-covered, highly embroidered feather beds.

As we approached the dungeon, the strains of Sigerson's violin music became audible. The King indicated I was to be placed in Sigerson's cell.

"Ask him to teach you something about music. You would be a capital fellow—as you British say—if you had a soul."

The barred door clanged behind me. The King stood for a long time and looked wistfully at Sigerson. "You could be free."

Sigerson abruptly turned his back to the King and walked toward the far wall of the cell. I thought he would have done well to behave more humbly.

Ludwig turned on his heel and strode away. The sound

of banging doors rang out behind him as he withdrew down the corridor leading away from the dungeon.

"If his mood swings toward cruelty, I fear for you."

"Take heart," Sigerson replied, "I can open any lock—when I choose." No sooner had he uttered these very consoling words when two guards came and stood outside of our cell. They were armed with what appeared to be genuine battle-axes. Sigerson turned pale. "Who will take care of Holmes?" he asked.

I reminded him that the nurse was there, and that there was little to be done since nature must be allowed in this case to run its course.

As the hours passed, our guard was changed. Sigerson grew increasingly despondent. I recalled how I had seen his sister throw herself sobbing on Holmes's breast. It was not difficult to imagine Victor doing the same. I tried to chat to pass the time.

"Is your sister also musical?" I asked him.

He hesitated and then asked, "When did you see my sister?"

I explained that Holmes had met her in Hundig's hut and that I had happened to see her through the window. I did not tell him how distressed she had seemed.

"How did you know it was my sister?"

"Of course the resemblance is remarkable," I said. "Holmes told me you had lent her your clothes."

"Holmes told you that?"

"We have very few secrets from each other," I explained.

"Quite so," he replied and paced about in our cell. After some time, Sigerson took up the violin and played, adding his music to the dripping rain. Thunder crackled an accompaniment and the lightning glared. I wished that I could check on Holmes's condition.

Progressively Sigerson's airs became more melancholy, much as Holmes's did when his mind wandered over alternatives in an unsolved case. Gloom gathered in the cell and except for the flashes of lightning it was difficult to see. I heard a door bang in the distance, and then another, closer to our cell. As the sounds of slammed doors resounded in the corridor, I became convinced that we were about to receive a royal visitor.

Sigerson rested the violin on his knee. He appeared calm, but I knew he was worried.

The keys rattled in the door and it was flung open—revealing Louis XIV. Behind his head a servant held up a many-branched candelabra. The chestnut wig tumbled in grand disorder, and the stiff collars of the royal cloak rose almost to his eyes. He indicated the silver candelabra be placed on the floor of the cell and then dismissed the servant and all the guards.

Sigerson and I both rose and bowed to His Highness. He stood back from the circle of light, the candlelight gleaming on his resplendent satin costume.

He pointed a gloved finger at Sigerson and said, "You! Come with me."

I stepped forward and said, "I demand to be released. I came here as an ambassador from the court of Queen Victoria. I shall not be ignored, confined, or treated rudely—nor shall my friend!"

The King left our cell and looked down the long corridor as though to see if we were observed. In the

outrageous costume, though he appeared thoroughly de-
mented, he was quite the most imperial figure I had ever
seen. At least there was no talk of mutilation.

The King spoke condescendingly to Sigerson: "Do you
value your life?"

It seemed that Sigerson took an eon to reply. When he
spoke it was with a certain insouciance, "Do you value
yours?"

With an imperturbable eye, he seemed to measure the
King—almost to challenge him. It was certainly all bluff,
for Sigerson was slender, tall, and rather fragile looking.

"Then you must teach me to play the violin," the King
commanded.

"Gladly," Sigerson responded, and he picked up the
instrument. "What would you learn?"

"Oh, the same that you were playing earlier. The waltz
tune your confederate hummed before the kiosk."

I was quite startled and alarmed by this casual reference
to Holmes's signal of several days before.

Sigerson played a bit of the tune, and then he handed
the violin to the Sun-King. Louis played no more than two
measures when Sigerson threw himself upon the majestic
figure, hugging him, it seemed, and shouting, "Holmes!"

"So it is," said a familiar voice from the splendid costume.

He threw aside the high-collared cloak and then
removed the curly Bourbon wig. Now I clearly perceived
the profile of the world's only consulting detective.

"Didn't you recognize me, Watson?" he asked crisply,
holding out his hand, which I shook over and over. I was
so delighted to see him quite his old self again, fully
enjoying a dramatic moment, that I could not even think

of scolding him for frightening me. But Sigerson up-braided him roundly in a high and piping voice.

Holmes had awakened shortly after I had been sum-moned by the King. He had easily persuaded Ilse to gather information for him about my prolonged absence during the afternoon, while he ate and regained something of his strength. "I should really have been at a loss without the good Ilse," he said. "She seems to have taken quite a fancy to you, Watson, but then the fair sex was always your department. I suppose I should apologize for appearing as the Sun-King, but it allowed the guards, even as you did, to assume I was Ludwig. What did you do, Watson, to incur the wrath of the King?"

I reported that I had failed to hum a snitch of Wagnerian opera.

Just then, we heard the footsteps of a person running in the corridor. I offered Holmes the wig, but he shook his head. "None of the hirelings would dare to reappear after my orders to leave the area. This will be one of our friends."

Holmes was quite correct. In the doorway, perspiration darkening his blond hair, Welcker appeared.

"Thank God you've recovered," he said to Holmes, panting. "You must save the King at once!"

"Pray explain yourself."

"He has gained the key to the high tower. He's standing there on the encirclement, in the storm. He may jump."

I looked at Holmes's pale face. How could this man demand aid from Holmes! Why did not he himself stand on the parapet with the King!

"His state of mind?" Holmes asked.

"Irrational, totally mad."

✠ 6 ✠

TO THE HIGH TOWER

"WE MUST PLAY to his game," Holmes said, and he donned the cloak and wig. The four of us quickly left the dungeon. When we came to the turn for the infirmary, Holmes ordered Sigerson to remain behind, which he did. Not a man for high adventure, I observed to myself.

Holmes and I followed Welcker through the maze of corridors and up many flights of stairs. The steps spiralled up the high tower as though they were rising to heaven. Finally Welcker stopped. He took Holmes's hand and said, "I cannot go further. I am so afraid of heights that I would faint in a matter of minutes."

Holmes glanced at me; I nodded, and we began rapidly to ascend.

The walls of the tower were pierced with windows, and through the windows came flashes of lightning. As we climbed ever higher, we saw the other towers and roofs of the castle diminishing below us. The wind gusted strongly, and at one point, when we stopped to rest, I felt the tower swaying.

Holmes was in no condition for this strenuous stair-climbing, and I prevailed on him to lean upon me. At first he refused, but before we were halfway up he was obliged to place his hand on my shoulder. We climbed again, but more slowly. Our footsteps echoed in the tower, the thunder resounded, and the rain beat against the windows. I saw that Holmes was beginning to sweat in his weakened condition, and I offered to carry the wig, but he refused.

Finally, just below the pointed roof, we saw a door. It had been left ajar, and rain now poured into the tower. Holmes explained, "Perhaps as a ghostly incarnation of Louis xiv, I shall simply be able to order him to return to his apartments. You must try your best to stay out of sight."

Even above the uproar of the storm, we could hear Ludwig declaiming his proclamation of love for the Bavarian people. We judged his position on the balcony to be such that he would not see us move through the door. The instant we stepped into the weather, we were drenched. The footing on the wet stones was extremely treacherous, but there was a little bannister about waist high, and I felt that even if we slipped we would not tumble over.

Holmes began to address Ludwig in French. Ludwig was not at all surprised to see one of his patrons in the flesh. The lightning cracked about us on all sides, and I developed some fear of being struck. The earth seemed miles below us. Suddenly I heard Holmes shouting, *"Non! Non!"* I peeked around the curved wall of the tower to see that Ludwig was now standing up on the bannister. He was flapping his arms and inviting Holmes, or rather Louis, to fly with him, like two swans.

Much to my horror, Holmes stepped upon the balustrade with him and held his hand. I could see that Holmes was speaking earnestly to him, as one wise king might to another. Apparently the touch of Holmes's hand was not pleasing to Ludwig, and he seemed to try to pull back. I saw Holmes was bracing himself. Illusion be damned! I was just about to step out and grab Holmes's other hand when I heard a new, feminine voice in the rain.

On the other side of Holmes and Ludwig, standing on the parapet, appeared the figure of Marie Antoinette. I rubbed my eyes in disbelief. It was as if she had materialized from air. And yet she seemed as real, standing in the rain and lightning, as Holmes or Ludwig. She wore an enormous jewelled crown and a high white wig. A ruff of lace encircled her graceful throat. The wind tried to catch her voluminous skirt like a sail. She smiled, then opened her fan to cover her smile. Coaxingly, she spoke to the King and invited him to go down the stairs with her to the Petit Trianon. She began to circle the tower, carefully placing her feet on the stones of the ledge, but laughing coyly and telling the King not to come too fast, that it would frighten her. Finally she stepped down from the bannister and held out her hand. Slowly Ludwig, too, descended and stood safely on the floor of the balcony.

Holmes followed Ludwig, and I moved my position so that they could walk toward the door without seeing me. Could this be Ilse, dressed as Marie Antoinette? It was not Ilse's nose. This was an arched, aristocratic nose. The Queen held her lace fan before her for a moment and then the fan disappeared into thin air.

"Spirit queen," Ludwig invoked.

Sleight of hand! It must be Sigerson. Quick wit, he had stayed behind for this. Probably the good Ilse had helped him find the King's costume closet, just as she had helped Holmes. And he had not hesitated to dress as a woman.

When Marie Antoinette backed into the door, the King seemed to spring at her, and they toppled backwards onto the inner landing. Holmes and I rushed in. The King collapsed. The Queen's wig was knocked off and it disappeared down the stairwell. Sigerson, hampered by the heavy dress, did his best to keep the King from tumbling down the stairs. Holmes and I quickly aided him.

"My dear fellow," Holmes said to Sigerson, "my life was in your hands."

Holmes was never effusive in his thanks, but it was clear he ranked Sigerson's courage very highly, and so did I.

It took nearly an hour for the three of us to carry the unconscious King down the stairs. Holmes was weak from illness; Sigerson had but puny physical strength for all his courage, and so we had a difficult descent. Eventually we entrusted Ludwig, still in a faint, to his faithful Welcker. On the floor at the bottom of the stairs, I found the white wig of Marie Antoinette and thought soberly of the enormous distance the thing had fallen.

Holmes, Sigerson, and I hurried away. As soon as we reached the infirmary, Holmes insisted that I rest, knowing I had borne the brunt of the King's weight.

Exhausted, I stretched myself fully clothed on the little narrow bed. The rain had ceased, but sheets of lightning still shook in the sky. Holmes and Sigerson gathered up dry cushions and retreated through French doors to the balcony, where they sat talking at a round wicker table. Through the doors, just before I closed my eyes, I registered the satin knee-britches of Louis xiv and the voluminous and shining skirt of Marie Antoinette. As sleep flickered over my brain, the fearful image of Holmes standing beside Ludwig on the parapet of the high tower flashed before me, and then the startling appearance of Marie Antoinette, like a guardian angel.

My dreams were troubled that night and laced with strands of overheard conversation. I heard Sigerson, though I dreamed it was his twin sister, explain, "My loyalty is to beauty, not war."

Holmes replied, "Why *any* Bavarian loyalty? You are, after all, English."

Sigerson said something to the effect that nurture as much as nature accounted for an individual's disposition.

Holmes snorted, "I'm a geneticist to the end." Then I dreamed for awhile that Holmes was a medical colleague of mine back in old St. Christopher's. "Genetics define the future."

Thunder rumbled in my illusion and with it sentences of political speculation. Sigerson said dreamily, ". . . architectural fantasies. Ludwig represents an alternative to the Prussian war machine."

Holmes demurred as though this explanation itself were too visionary.

Sigerson said, "Prussia could engulf all of Europe in a war. Your England would not be exempt." His voice was like a spike.

In my mind's eye I saw an army of uniformed and helmeted men, and then they were replaced with peasants, dressed softly in hues of brown and tan, tunics daubed with images of swans.

"Yes, she loved music," Holmes said in a tone that I had never heard before.

"The violin?" Sigerson asked; he seemed to be crying.

I dreamed that Marie Antoinette transmogrified into a swan sitting on the bannister of the balcony. Holmes kissed the swan's forehead, and she enveloped him in her shining wings.

When I awoke, it was because Holmes was gently shaking my shoulder.

"They have taken the King," he said.

"Who has taken him?" I responded sleepily.

"Dr. Gudden and eight assistants, backed up by the Chief of the Munich police and his armed lieutenants."

Welcker and Count Dürckheim had already left to follow them. Holmes had gotten all the information from Osterholzer, the coachman, who had stayed behind.

The Munich Commission had come in the dead of night. They had succeeded in replacing the castle guard with their own men.

"They've gone to Berg," Sigerson added. "It's a small castle on Lake Starnberg." Then he paused and looked first at Holmes and then at me.

"I doubt we can help him now," I said.

"We ought merely to go to London," Holmes said, "—all three of us."

Sigerson paced up and down in a way reminiscent of

Holmes himself when he was vexed or wrestling with some puzzle.

Finally Sigerson said, "You must return without me."

"But why?" I asked.

"There are many reasons," Sigerson said softly.

"I thought we had discussed everything," Holmes said. "You can have a fine career in London."

Sigerson shook his head. "I do not wish to disappoint you," he said carefully, "but it is not right that I should go with you."

"Remember in the hut," Holmes said rather mysteriously, "you promised to leave with us."

"Did I?" said Sigerson. "I think my sister promised for me, didn't she? I can scarcely be bound by her words."

Holmes turned to me. "Forgive me, my dear Watson, but I wonder if you would allow me to talk with our friend in private?"

I prepared to leave, but Sigerson called me back.

"Wait, Dr. Watson. Pray do not leave us. Mr. Holmes, we have already had our private chat. I do not wish another."

I stood there, rather foolishly I'm afraid, looking at the two men. Each spoke with such imperial and icy command that they seemed to be mirror images of each other.

Suddenly Holmes shrugged.

"I have always known it to be an error to express any emotional concern for clients," he said.

"I am not your client," Sigerson said. "You came here to aid Ludwig."

"I suppose it seems so."

Holmes had become alarmingly pale. And yet I could

not understand exactly why. It really was not necessary to insist upon the young violinist leaving Bavaria for safety's sake. Only the King threatened him. Let him return to Munich and do as he liked, I thought.

"Since you have abandoned the King," Sigerson said, "I must use what powers I have to help him."

"You only place yourself in jeopardy," Holmes said.

"I am my own keeper." Sigerson turned on his heel and left the infirmary.

Holmes lay down on his little cot, folded his arms across his chest, and closed his eyes. "Allegiance to a diseased imagination is itself a disease."

When I stood at the window, I noticed Sigerson crossing the courtyard. I watched for some time, and in a quarter of an hour, I saw a small coach pass under the portals of Neuschwanstein and onto the paved-stone road that led down the mountain. I roamed around the castle for an hour or so while Holmes rested. Then I called for lunch to be delivered to the infirmary, and Holmes and I sat out on the balcony in wicker chairs at the round table.

The very air surrounding the castle seemed robbed of the spirit that had animated it. Ludwig the Swan-Prince was taken into captivity. Could such a swan survive in a cage? Whatever confinement to which Dr. Gudden sentenced him would certainly seem to be a cage. I said as much to Holmes, but Holmes was not in a communicative mood.

We decided to spend yet another night at the castle, and then to leave early in the morning to begin our journey back to London.

❧ 7 ❧

A FATEFUL DAY
IN BAVARIA

THE MORNING OF June 13, 1886, dawned grey and misty in Bavaria. Holmes had obviously spent a very bad night, though I had slept exceedingly well—no troubled dreams of politics and armies. His face was drawn, and he appeared hypersensitive and nervous.

"You've scarcely slept," I observed.

"A brilliant deduction," he replied sarcastically.

"This weather somewhat reminds me of certain spring days at home," I said amiably.

"Except for the fact that normally you do not wake up in a castle, surrounded by mountains and lakes."

I saw that further efforts at civil conversation would only be scorned, and so I held my peace.

After an interval, Holmes spoke out. "The truth of the matter is that I'm not quite ready to leave. I think that we shall have to go to Berg to make one more attempt."

"Really?" I said. "An attempt to accomplish what, if I may ask?"

"Of course you may," Holmes said meekly, and I saw that his new tone was offered as an apology for his earlier churlishness. "We came to Bavaria to help the King and to save Victor Sigerson from danger. We have accomplished neither. Therefore, we will now leave for Berg, survey the scene, and then determine if other courses of action are open to us."

I was rather surprised to hear Holmes announce a change of plans. It was not characteristic of him. Usually only some new piece of information could cause him to alter his course, and I was sure no message had come in the night. Perhaps the blow to the head and his prolonged unconsciousness were yet having some effect on his usual decisiveness.

We found Osterholzer at the stable and had no difficulty in securing a small carriage pulled by two bay horses. He again offered to drive.

As we left Neuschwanstein, I could not resist looking back. The white towers gleamed wetly. I regarded the tiny balcony encircling the high tower and thought how only recently we had stood there in the dark with the lightning flashing around us. Slowly mist enfolded the turrets, then the towers and lower walls. The castle itself was dissolving into airy nothingness. I looked ahead at the winding road that took our carriage down into the valley, and I listened to the wet clop of horses' hooves on the roadbed.

We spent most of the day riding through rain and mist from Neuschwanstein toward the little castle on Lake Starnberg where the King had been taken. As the day wore on, I could see Holmes was quite fatigued, and I worried again about his health. I insisted that we stop at a village inn for a hot lunch. The people at the tavern were all speaking of the new Regency established under Ludwig's Uncle Luitpold. Holmes sat upright at the table but with his eyes closed. I thought he was asleep, but he opened his eyes when a plate of Wiener schnitzel was placed before him. "You notice, no doubt," he said to me, "that no one hints at the King's dissipation. No one complains about his obsession with music or his mania for building." Then Holmes turned his attention to cutting his food into invalid-sized pieces. "Does their restraint surprise you?" he asked me. Not wishing to tax Holmes with chatter, I remained silent and listened to the talk of the tavern. The country folk foresaw a unified Germany dominated by Bismarck.

By the time we reached the village near Berg castle, Holmes was so weak that Osterholzer had to help him into the inn, where we engaged a room. But as soon as the groom left, Holmes took a deep breath, as though he would inhale strength from the air, and said, "Now, Watson, to the castle."

Since it was raining slightly, we borrowed umbrellas from the innkeeper and walked—Holmes moving as best he could—toward Berg Castle. It was small and charming, like a gingerbread toy, yet I noticed that there were bars on the lower windows. Like all the Bavarian lakes, Starnberg was a lovely body of water and its proximity to the immaculate castle grounds made the place seem even more picturesque. Holmes was silent during our walk. At some distance out in the water, I saw the island that Osterholzer had told me was named Roseninsel, so named because fifteen thousand rose trees had been planted there. In the midst of the scented island was one of Ludwig's pavilion retreats. It seemed to me I could smell something of the roses in the damp air.

At the door of the castle, Holmes asked the servant to bring Victor Sigerson to us, and in a moment the violinist stood before us.

"You have disobeyed me," Sigerson said to Holmes. "Come into this room, please."

We followed him downstairs to a kind of boot room. It had a small barred window, no glass, set high in the wall, just above ground level.

Holmes began, "I entreat you—"

"You have already entreated me. I don't have time to speak with you. I'm about to take a stroll with His Majesty." Sigerson walked to the window through which a small section of the garden and lake were visible. "Come here," he said to Holmes.

Holmes walked to Sigerson and took the hand that Sigerson stretched out to him. With a movement so rapid that I could only register its results, Sigerson handcuffed Holmes to a bar of the window!

"What have you done!" Holmes thundered.

Sigerson answered, "I have detained you."

Holmes replied, "I daresay I am your equal in opening locks."

"My dear man," Sigerson responded mildly, "do you think I would underestimate you? This is no ordinary lock, but one I have built myself. Farewell. Now you shall have peace."

Before I could say a word, he deserted us, Holmes manacled to the bar of the window. Immediately with his free hand, Holmes produced a wire from his pocket and inserted it into the lock of the handcuff. With an expression of supreme concentration, he probed the interior of the lock.

"May I be of assistance?"

"Quiet," Holmes murmured. He listened to tiny sounds from within the lock.

Through the high window, I could see the King, Sigerson, and Dr. Gudden walking through the garden. Holmes took only a moment from his work to glance out the window. "Report their activities," he said, focusing his attention on his work.

I replied that an argument had just broken out between the three men. The King pointed toward the lake. Dr. Gudden took out a pair of handcuffs. Ludwig became more agitated, and Sigerson spoke into the King's ear. Gudden braceleted them together, but immediately they began to run toward the lake, leaving Gudden watching. "What are they doing?" I asked in amazement.

"The lock is impossible," Holmes exclaimed.

"Surely not," I said.

Through the window we watched Sigerson and the King, linked at the wrists, splashing into the water. They began to swim awkwardly.

Holmes rattled the locked handcuffs against the bars. "Stop them!" he shouted at me.

I ran from the room and out of the castle. As I rushed into the garden I saw that Sigerson and the King, far out in the water, were floundering. Gudden flung off his overcoat and sprang into the waves. He quickly reached them. What happened next was difficult to tell. The three struggled together in the water. I hurried down the path toward the lake.

But suddenly an enormous snowy swan blocked my way. With white wings hoisted like sails, it stretched its neck and hissed. Uncertainly, I stepped forward. Five feet tall and five feet wide, the swan was a gate of feathers closed against me. I tried to go around, but the cob aggressively preceded me. Its eyes were angry, and its beak snapped resoundingly. Scooping up gravel from the pathway, I pelted it. The white feathers armored its breast, and the pebbles bounced away.

The swan began to move toward me. I was forced to take a step in retreat. Its head seemed to stretch even higher and resembled the hood of a cobra such as I had encountered in India. Suddenly the cob struck my thigh. Through the cloth of my trousers, the beak fastened into my flesh and twisted. Blood soaked the fabric. As soon as I fell backwards, the bird was upon me. Its webbed feet trod my chest; its toenails penetrated my shirt.

The feathers of its breast covered my face like a horrible cloud, and I shoved against it futilely. Finally I rolled from beneath the swan and scrambled to my feet. My blood besmirched the white feathers of its breast and splotched the pinions of one wing. Still the cob clacked at me and held its knobbed wings outspread, like a gargoyle. I picked up two handsful of gravel, yelled, and charged the swan, aiming at its head from both sides in a cross-fire. This time the bird folded its wings and scuttled behind an ornamental boulder.

I ran toward the water, but the three men had disappeared.

The rain pattered into the lake. The King's hat lay on the shore. I waded out into the water. I stood there while waves lapped around my thighs, but I saw no turbulence farther out or any other hint that might have oriented me in my rescue attempt.

Thoroughly sodden, I left the water and stood on a stone bench. I hoped to see someone swimming toward the shore. I felt stunned. Had I dreamed the entire scene? In swallowing up the three, the lake seemed to have swallowed reality. I walked sadly back to the castle.

Every step of the way I dreaded bringing the news to Holmes. Perhaps he had seen the drowning. My thigh was throbbing, and I felt sick with cold.

The instant I walked into the room, I saw the lock fall from Holmes's wrist. A free man, Holmes turned to me and whispered, "Sigerson is dead."

I nodded.

"And the King."

"Drowned," I replied.

"Help me," Holmes said quietly.

Supporting his weight, I assisted him out of the castle, through the dripping garden, and back to our inn. When I put Holmes to bed, he asked me to leave him.

In my own room, I washed the blood from my thigh and changed my clothes. Both Holmes and I were ill for several days.

During my recuperation, I learned that a fisherman had found the bodies of both Dr. Gudden and Ludwig out in the lake. Gudden was found with the King's coat in his grasp; his face was cut and marked and his throat showed bruises suggesting that he had been partially strangled.

Apparently there had been a violent struggle among them. The body of Sigerson was never recovered.

No official mention of Victor Sigerson was ever made, and Holmes decided that it was unnecessary to report that Sigerson had gone into the water with Ludwig and Gudden.

When we were about to check out, the innkeeper said that he had a letter for us that had been mislaid for several days.

Holmes and I sat down on either side of the small fire in the inn's sitting room. Holmes slowly opened the envelope. "The letter is dated the twelfth of June." His eyes passed over the page. His hands shook.

When he looked at me again! Never had his eyes seemed more cold and reptilian. He told me that Sigerson had had a sense of his impending death and that he wished to give his Stradivarius to Holmes. That he had sent the violin to Munich and that he wished for us a life of happiness.

"The name at the end," Holmes said, "is simply V. Sigerson." For a moment, Holmes's eye held mine.

I shook my head. "How could he possibly have guessed we would come to Berg?" I asked.

"V. Sigerson," Holmes folded the note and placed it in his breast pocket. "A mind without equal." He rose abruptly and walked to the fireplace, where he stood nudging the toe of his boot against the single log of the little summer fire.

When we arrived in Munich, Holmes fetched the Stradivarius, as Sigerson had directed. Soon we were headed north from Munich on the train. Holmes stood the violin case on its end, clamped between his knees. He was silent and morose, yet he seemed somehow settled and resigned. Strangely, Sigerson had said that Holmes would find peace. I felt he would improve further once we were back in familiar surroundings.

As we clacked over the rails, Holmes put his hand over the snub-nosed end of the case and spoke.

"I could almost regard this whole adventure as a kind of midsummer night's nightmare," he said, "if it were not for this." He paused and tapped the hard case. "'What fools we mortals be.'" His voice was sad. Speaking of the instrument, he added, "I will treasure it."

For a long time afterwards, whenever Sherlock Holmes played the violin, the ghostly towers of Neuschwanstein rose in my mind, as did the visage of the madly becurled King Ludwig II, whom we had failed to save.

❧ IV ❧

THE
PRESENT

THE WOMAN IN RED
PAYS A CALL

THE ADVENTURE OF the Mad King occurred thirty-six years ago. It was never published, nor had I even read it for decades. Forgotten. I felt numbed by the story. Sigerson was dead, and yet—I little knew what sense to make of things. It seemed as though my mind were being softly covered by a blanket of cold. What should I do now? And tomorrow?

Holmes had loved and lost. My sorrow for him swept back through time. Again, he seemed to sit across from me on the train, tapping the violin case he held between his knees: "I will treasure it."

I sat before the dying fire and listened. I heard footsteps in the corridor below. Yes, I distinctly heard a quiet slippered footstep on the staircase. Nannerl? I dreaded seeing those cold grey eyes. How could I explain that I meant her no harm? But who was she? The twin sister of Sigerson was merely Holmes's fabrication. Violet and Victor Sigerson were surely one and the same. They were—she was—dead. Suppose it was from some other corner of Holmes's life, entirely, from which Nannerl was emerging? I imagined her every step, and when just the right interval had passed to bring my visitor to my door, I spoke in a loud, calm voice.

"Won't you come in?"

In she stepped. Not the gnarled Nannerl. But the woman in red, her white hair waving softly about her pretty face. Dressed in her warm, fur-trimmed cloak, a sprig of holly on the collar, she seemed not to have felt the cold at all.

First I locked the door behind her and then I bowed. "Madame, I am at your service. But I cannot guess your identity."

"You have written about me in the past."

"Memory fails me," I was obliged to say.

"And yet my photograph, long treasured by Holmes, is in this room."

As she walked across the room to the desk upon which sat her photograph, I quickly said, "Irene Adler, *the* woman."

She picked up the photograph and held it beside her face so that I might compare the two.

"'Age cannot wither you nor custom stale your infinite variety,'" I said.

She smiled. "How kind of you to sit up for me, Dr. Watson."

"How kind of you to call in this weather," I replied as I pulled a chair close to the fire for her. I beat the log with a poker and made the sparks fly up.

I indicated my stack of books with a gesture and asked, "Have you been here before today?"

"No, no," she said. "That is the work of Nannerl."

"May I fix you something hot to drink?"

"Yes," she said, "please."

I busied myself making us both a cup of hot chocolate. Indicating the closed folder bearing the title "The Adventure of the Mad King," she said cheerfully, "I see that you have spent Christmas Eve reading about Bavaria."

"And a strange tale it was, too. Fancy all the time I was with Holmes in Bavaria, I thought him to be concerned about the King and a violinist whom I thought to be male."

"And now?" she asked.

"Now I know the violinist to have been a woman."

Irene Adler sipped her chocolate and contemplated me with steady blue eyes. As is sometimes the case with older women who have white hair, her eyes were fascinating spots of colour. She looked seriously at me for a moment.

"I have always had the greatest admiration for Mr. Holmes," she said slowly. "How do you think it was that I was able to elude him and the King of Bohemia? How was it that I was able to arrange for Godfrey Norton—God rest his soul—and for myself to elude the net set by the great detective?"

"Why, I don't know," I said honestly.

"I knew a great deal about Mr. Holmes. Unlike most criminals, which I never was, of course, I did not under-estimate his intelligence. I knew a great deal about him *before* I came to London. I felt that I had an *intimate* knowledge of how his mind worked. How would I gain such knowledge, Dr. Watson?"

"Indeed, I cannot guess," I said. "Perhaps from my tales?"

She sat down again, and then she smiled trustingly at

me before she continued. "I learned a great deal about him from Violet Sigerson."

I merely stared at her.

Her eyelids dropped and she looked into the fire before glancing back at me. "You can rely on me, Dr. Watson, to keep a secret. But it was she, and not I, who outsmarted Sherlock Holmes."

"In the matter of the Bohemian scandal?"

"And in the matter of Lake Starnberg. Her knowledge of him was used entirely for his benefit—an enormous sacrifice on her part."

I seated myself across the fire from Irene Adler. She was very composed. Much of the hauteur of her bearing as an opera-singer had softened into simplicity and kindness.

"I feel that you have much to tell me," I said. "But please take your time. Be comfortable. Very willingly shall I listen. I perceive that there is some sequel to the Bavarian adventure. I have just read my own manuscript, but I cannot conceive what the sequel may be."

She set aside her cup, clasped her hands in her lap, and leaned toward me.

"First of all, let me say that only two people drowned in Lake Starnberg on June 13, 1886, and those two people were Ludwig II and Dr. Gudden. Violet Sigerson did not drown." With a candid expression, she added, "It happened that in 1886 I often travelled with the King of Bohemia."

At this frank statement, I became embarrassed and shifted my gaze from the wedgewood eyes of Irene Adler. She noticed my discomfort.

"Please, Dr. Watson," she said in an understanding but firm tone. "Let us not be so terribly Victorian. To be more exact, I was the mistress of the King of Bohemia at that time."

I forced myself to look again at her face, for I knew that she would not go on with the story unless I acknowledged these facts unashamedly. She smiled patiently at me.

"As you may remember," she continued, "I was a rather well-known opera singer in those days. I had always wanted to sing at the Munich Opera or in the private theatre of the Residenz for the King of Bavaria. Everyone knew that Ludwig had become eccentric by this time. It was said that he had become enamoured of realistic effects. If the script called for a rainstorm, the singers were made to perform in actual rain. He would have the roof of the theatre rolled back. Some say that he staged degenerate tortures during his final days, but I did not believe that. It was true that often a very lavish production would be mounted for him alone. Most singers were quite disconcerted to sing to a hall absolutely empty except for the King.

"I knew that I did not wish to sing for Ludwig without my own protector present, and so I persuaded the King of Bohemia, who would have given me anything at that time, to visit his neighbour in Bavaria. In June of 1886, we were in Munich. We heard that Ludwig was away at some of his other castles—I believe they thought him to be at Hohenschwangau, but actually he was at Linderhof and then at Neuschwanstein. Anyway, we thought we would wait at Munich for his return.

"As it turned out, we never saw him alive, though we reverently visited his body during the days that it lay in Michaels-Kirche.

"But I get ahead of myself. During the time that we were waiting in Munich for Ludwig's return, we heard much about a little island, the Roseninsel, on Lake Starnberg, an island covered with roses. As you know, the lake is not far from Munich.

"The King of Bohemia was well acquainted with the Duchess Ludovica, whose daughter Elizabeth had been a good friend of Ludwig's. It was an easy matter for my King of Bohemia to call upon the Duchess, and, using one of her boats and her people, for us to visit the scented island Roseninsel.

"Both the King of Bohemia and I fell in love with the island. We even sent the boat away with orders for it not to return until two weeks had passed. We kept a few of our own servants to cook for us and so forth, but otherwise we were quite alone.

"While such arrangements often start out idyllically enough, it is easy for two people who are used to the company of the world to grow weary of each other in isolation. The weather changed, too, from wonderfully warm sun to a chilly rain.

"It became my main pleasure to walk alone around the perimeter of the island, even in the rain. On June 13, as I took one of these solitary walks, I found a woman, half-drowned, half-dead with fatigue, her face scratched and half her clothes torn away, washed up on the island. I wrapped her in my own shawl and ran back to fetch some servants. Soon we had her warm and dry inside the pavilion.

"I was struck from the beginning by how quick she was at making inferences, and she lost no time in supposing that only royalty of some degree would be found in housekeeping on Ludwig's island. She begged me not to let anyone else see her. Because it meant so much to her, I was more than willing to oblige.

"She did not seem to me to be entirely of stable mind. Of course I knew that anyone who had come close to drowning would likely be nervous for some days to come, but she seemed to suffer from some ill-defined grief. Often she sat in a sort of melancholy stupor. I found her case to be interesting. At least she was more interesting than the King, who had become a thorough bore. He had taken up fishing to pass the time while we awaited the return boat, and that kept him occupied for hours. So I had a great deal of time to talk with this young woman.

"I remarked to her once how extraordinary it was that her hair was cropped short, like a man's, and that she had been wearing a man's trousers. When I mentioned the trousers, she began to cry. It occurred to me that they probably reminded her of someone who was dear to her. I asked if she had been alone in the fishing boat, or if her husband or lover had perhaps been lost. She replied, 'He is lost to me forever.'

"Several evenings later I had a fire built in her room, and I told her to lay her head in my lap. I smoothed her forehead and stroked her cropped hair, and eventually I asked her again why her hair was short.

"This time she gazed up at me with her fine grey eyes and said, 'My hair is short because often in the world I have passed myself off as a man.'

"Here was a circumstance that delighted and intrigued me. Naturally I would not rest until I heard the whole story, but I did not try to extract it all that night. I thought it best to be cautious with her. I had seen how unstable were her emotions. I was not wrong in my estimate, for she truly was precariously balanced.

"At last the boat came, and we were able to leave Roseninsel. Of course we heard from the people on the boat that Ludwig had been drowned in the lake during our stay on the island. As soon as I heard that Ludwig had drowned on the same day that she had washed ashore, I suspected that their stories must be intertwined. Finally, one day, I asked her if she had been Ludwig's lover. Again, she began to sob and to deny vehemently that Ludwig had ever touched her. I tried to reassure her and to tell her that I believed her, but she hung her head much of the day, as though it were sunk in shame.

"Another day I asked her if we ought not notify someone that she was alive and well. Had she no friend or family whose anxiety should be relieved? She replied, 'My friend . . . thinks I am dead. I have arranged it that way.'

" 'But why?' I persisted. 'Why have you played so cruel a deception?'

"She replied in a kind of wonderment: 'If I had not done so, I would now be his lover,' and then she added so softly I could scarcely hear her, 'or his wife.'

"I took her hand and pressed it in my own. I could see that I must not ask her for further explanation at that time. Though I was not and am not a conventional person, I was surprised. Why not be the man's lover, if she so loved him?"

Irene Adler paused in her narrative.

I said, "This, then, was Violet Sigerson." She nodded. "She must have thought," I went on, "that if Holmes believed her to be dead that he would grieve and then naturally experience a lessening of grief over time."

"Yes," Irene said. "That is what she did think."

"But we saw her drown."

"Violet Sigerson had many talents," Irene explained. "Sometimes she earned extra money by giving magic shows—"

"Yes," I interrupted. "Indeed, I saw one of her shows in Edinburgh."

"With her skill as an escape artist she was able to get free of the handcuffs that shackled her to Ludwig. Apparently it is not uncommon for magicians to carry some of their paraphernalia on their person."

I remembered how even Holmes had always carried his wire.

Miss Adler went on, "She thought that Holmes would be watching for some sign of her swimming, and so she swam almost entirely underwater."

I recalled the choppy water of the lake and how cold it had been. Violet Sigerson could easily have been really drowned in the lake. She had risked a very great deal to make Holmes believe she had died. But why? Why?

"Of course, she did not dare return to her place as Victor Sigerson with the Munich Opera Orchestra. She feared Holmes would check."

For a moment Irene was silent and then she continued.

"Since I knew many people in the musical world, I was able to get Violet a place in the Paris Opera Orchestra. Even though she now had a job—again, disguised as a male—she was not happy." Irene seemed fatigued by the memory.

"Once when I left Paris for a short while, I returned to find Violet sitting in our rooms, smoking a pipe, dressed like Sherlock Holmes. At first I treated it as a lark. I think that both Holmes and Violet had an unusual penchant for disguises. I myself have used them at times."

I recalled that in 1887, Irene Adler had spoken to Holmes and me at our door in disguise. Holmes had thought the voice familiar, as I noted in "A Scandal in Bohemia," but we had not penetrated her disguise at the time.

"And so I was not unduly alarmed," she went on, "by Violet's dressing as Holmes. But, you see, it became her preferred costume. I began to believe that it was an unhealthy way of possessing him. She had given him up by sacrificing her own identity; now she sought to have him by assuming his identity. She adopted his mannerisms. It was during this period that I learned a great deal about Holmes. But I saw that Violet needed medical aid. At length, I broached the subject to her.

"She was much more reasonable than one might have anticipated. She told me that she was tempted to let Holmes know that she had survived Lake Starnberg, and then she begged me never to let her approach him. I told her that she must take responsibility for that: I would not become her keeper. When I urged her to fulfill her obvious desire for the man, she became hysterical.

"Slowly she developed the idea that she wished to return to London and she wished to become a voluntary inmate of a mental hospital. We discussed it fairly rationally at times. Other times I could see that she harboured a fantasy that if she were locked in some jail-like structure, Holmes in the figure of Louis XIV would rescue her."

"But was she really so ill," I asked, "that she needed to stay in a hospital?"

Irene Adler sighed and smoothed her dress over her knees. Her face was mobile and expressive, and now she again looked old and full of regret.

"My life was made much more complicated at that time because I met Godfrey Norton. In other words, I fell in love. Violet took an instantaneous dislike of Godfrey and he of her. It made me quite sad, but I was unable to make either of them view the other with anything but jealous suspicion. To Violet, Godfrey was far too ordinary a person for me to love. I think the very normality of the attraction irritated her. She became so irascible at length that the thought of entrusting Violet to the care of someone else, by someone trained to do it, gave me great relief."

She looked up at me with her face full of grief and guilt.

"I'm sure that you had done far more for her than anyone else would have done," I said sincerely. "Holmes, too, was sometimes very difficult to live with. I left these lodgings more than once to marry, myself. I do his memory no harm by saying that he was often arrogant, demanding, and inconsiderate. Yet, in him these traits were balanced by others. Certainly he was not without warmth, for all his appearance of aloofness."

"Perhaps if Godfrey had come into my life at a later time, Violet would have regained enough equilibrium to have found him no threat. As it was . . ."

"But by your own account," I reminded her, "she had

already embedded herself in a world of irrational fantasies before Godfrey Norton appeared on the scene."

"Yes, that is true," Irene said. But she did not look satisfied.

"Here, have a bit of brandy," I said. "I often do when I'm sitting here alone late at night."

I fetched her a glass and she received it gratefully.

"I take it," I went on, "that Godfrey Norton has died?"

"Yes, he died ten years ago."

"You know, Holmes thought that *you* had died, years ago."

"When I retired from singing, I let it be thought that I was dead."

"And what became of Violet Sigerson?" I asked.

"Over the years, whenever I came to London, I visited her. Sometimes she was glad to see me. Other times she was morose or surly. Once she didn't know me. She has become increasingly irrational of late. I was afraid she might harm you, and so I sent you a warning note."

"And you wrote to Dr. Wiggins, asking him not to participate in my research."

She nodded and continued. "No lock can hold her. She has retained her skill as an escape-artist."

"Then she *is* the woman whom Dr. Wiggins and I know as Nannerl."

"Why in God's name, Dr. Watson, didn't they simply marry?"

I shook my head in bewilderment. I thought of Holmes's cold, passionless nature. Yet that was truly only a façade. No one knew better than I, especially after all that I had learned this day, that Holmes's emotions were merely controlled and concealed, not absent. If Violet had loved him, surely she knew as much.

There was a knock at the door.

"Who is it?" I asked.

"Dorothy."

"Who?"

"Fanny."

"What's going on?" I asked, rising from my chair.

"Augusta, Nannerl." As though by magic, the door—though I had turned the bolt—swung open.

"Violet!" Irene exclaimed, for there stood Nannerl—Violet Sigerson—dressed as Sherlock Holmes!

Irene immediately rose from her chair, passed in front of me, and embraced her. Violet appeared excited and confused, but not dangerous. Irene stepped back from Violet and examined her.

"You seem better," she said.

"Violet, Dorothy, Fanny, Augusta, Nannerl is . . . is . . . waiting now."

"Waiting for what?" My voice was more aggressive than I intended.

"I had . . ." Her voice trailed off.

"What did you have, dear?" Irene asked.

"I had . . . an idea." But she said nothing else.

"Please," I said. "Come in." She took a tentative step forward, crossed the room to the fireplace, touched the toe of the Persian slipper. I added cajolingly, "Please, let's chat a bit." We all sat down. "Tell me, why have you used these many names?"

Violet's mind seemed to focus itself.

"Who were these women?" she asked us.

Irene and I exchanged a glance.

Slowly, from I know not what dim corner of memory, emerged an odd fact: Dorothy was the name of the poet William Wordsworth's sister. "Augusta was the half-sister of Lord Byron," I blurted. "Fanny was the sister of John Keats."

"And Fanny Mendelssohn!" Irene added. "The talented sister of Felix."

"But Nannerl?" I asked.

"The sister of the greatest genius of them all," Irene said. "Wolfgang Amadeus Mozart."

Quietly I drew a sobering conclusion: "They were all the brilliant sisters of famous men."

"Naturally," Irene spoke with such sadness, "you could not marry your own brother."

"My half-brother. We shared the same musical mother."

Irene moved to embrace Violet, silently, for a long moment. "An impossible situation," Irene said.

The last night Holmes and I spent at Neuschwanstein rose in my memory. I had just read about it. While I slept restlessly in the infirmary, the figure of Marie Antoinette had transformed into a swan who folded Holmes in her wings. Violet. The chaste kiss Holmes left on her forehead. And they had been speaking, not of Marie Antoinette's love of music, but of their mother's; a brother telling his sister of a mother she had never known.

"And Sherlock knew," I said, "that you were his sister?"

"I realized it first," she said. Tears filled Violet's eyes, but she did not allow them to spill. "I tried to prevent his knowing. I took him off the case of my parentage. I was the hidden, illegitimate child, of course. He followed me to

Munich. I destroyed the evidence ahead of him, but then he simply deduced the truth. We acknowledged we loved each other. We discussed the alternatives."

"There were no alternatives," I said.

Irene spoke patiently, "There are always alternatives, Dr. Watson."

"Yes," Violet said. "After all, we did not grow up as siblings. We could have disregarded the truth."

"Never," I said.

"No," Irene said thoughtfully. "Sherlock was not a man to disregard the truth. In such matters, I'm sure he was quite conventional."

I thought of how in May of 1886, Sherlock had returned from Munich and lost himself to cocaine. How he had sat in this very room, enveloped in melancholia, trying to dispel the inner gloom with injection after injection. Certainly he had seen no remedy. Then Hornig had come to us and we were off to Neuschwanstein.

"Why have you come to me now?" I asked.

She had given me information that I could never have discovered.

Violet leaned close to my face. The area around her eyes was black, as though stage make-up had smudged. Her eyes seemed scorched. There was an artificial rose colour on her cheek. She looked like an aged woman of the night.

"I want it back," she said.

"What?" I asked. "The Stradivarius?" I felt Violet deserved to have the violin.

But Violet shook her head. "No, not the violin," she said. "My life."

Irene and I looked wonderingly at each other. Surely Irene's eyes were tracing the marks of the years on my face even as my eyes registered the touch of time upon her. And yet there were Irene's eyes; full of compassion, they could not have been more alive and beautiful, though the skin around them was creased and dry. She lowered her eyelids.

"We don't have youth to give," Irene said gently.

But Violet still regarded us expectantly.

"Why did you attack me?" It was difficult to imagine that the creature before me could have had the will to injure anyone.

"You were trying to protect Sherlock, weren't you, my dear?" Irene said. "His reputation."

"Never would I have revealed this," I asserted. "You could have simply spoken to me, written to me from St. Giles. My lips would have been sealed forever."

Now Violet studied my face. I saw tenseness leave her countenance. Something like trust crossed her face and then an expression I must call *peace* settled there. To my vast surprise, I saw she was going to ask something specific of me, was going to receive my answer—yes—no matter what her request.

"I do want it back," she said patiently, kindly.

My helplessness opened like an abyss at my feet. I could only stammer.

"How . . . how . . . impossible."

It was then I saw her kinship to Sherlock. She knew the answer! She was waiting for me to figure it out! How calm she looked! No trace of madness in her face. Just patience.

"Dr. Watson," she said crisply. "Would I ask the impossible of you?"

She crossed the room to the deal-top table where the violin case was lying among the old bottles of chemicals and empty flasks and beakers. With her back turned to us, she looked so like Holmes! She seemed as tall as Holmes. Would that she might turn—and there would be Holmes himself laughing at our acceptance of his most ingenious disguise, full of explanations!

But no.

Violet's hands moved among the flasks and chemicals. She picked up bottles and read labels. Abruptly she unscrewed a lid and held the jar under her nose. Whiffing the red powder, she remarked, "Still pungent."

She snapped the locks of the case. Her fingertips swept across the strings. There seemed no music there. The strings were flaccid. In a wink, she whisked the instrument under her chin and held it in that odd professional grip between the jaw and shoulder. With her hands, she tightened and rosined the bow and then, while playing near the tip of the bow, used her left hand to turn the pegs and tighten the strings. "And how have you spent your life, Dr. Watson?" she asked me.

"As a doctor," I replied.

"Yes. And . . ."

"As your brother's friend—"

"As his chronicler." Here she reached the interval of the fifth between each set of strings. Starting on the lowest string—the sound was full and rich—she tossed off a scale and ran up another and another, the sound softer and softer as she climbed; on the high string, her hand scampered after itself all the way up the fingerboard till the very highest and softest note was reached.

"I paid a visit to Dr. Wiggins's office," Violet said. "I was there much of the afternoon."

"What have you done?" I asked sternly.

"I read," she answered.

I could only stare at her. She placed the violin back in its case and approached me.

"Dr. Watson, I read your stories. Dr. Wiggins had left them out. I read a little about you, Irene. And it made me smile and rejoice in your intelligence. In our intelligence because I, like any reader, felt myself a part of the tale."

I flushed with pleasure. The old stories, my work of so long ago, had lasted, had succeeded.

"And, between the lines, Dr. Watson, I read of your generosity, your willingness to help my brother, to be his friend."

She came toward me, placed her hands on my shoulders, and quietly kissed my cheek. "You made my brother live again. I saw him and heard him in your words."

She drew back and looked so deeply within me, it was like a touch. And when she withdrew her gaze, she had left an idea behind.

"I can give you back your life, in some humble measure," I said, "by writing about you."

"I have decided that I wish to be included," she said simply. "Make me live."

❧ 2 ❧

AFTERWORD

THAT I HAVE tried to do so, you, dear reader, must attest. At that moment, I vowed that Violet's story would take form. That her skill, her courage, her heroic appearance as Marie Antoinette in the storm on the high tower of Neuschwanstein, her music—all of that would come before you.

Now I have written far into the night.

Violet ended that evening dramatically. She turned down the gas lamp, ignited the red powder from the chemical table, and played the violin like one possessed. She played the Bach "Chaconne" for us that had so bewitched Holmes. I remember yet how he stood beneath her open hotel window—not knowing who played—and lifted his face toward the sound of that piece which has so much of both heaven and earth in it. As Violet played for Irene and me, the odour of lilacs seemed in the air again, and I found myself impatient to greet the spring.

As a faithful chronicler, I must end on a sad note, and yet it is not entirely sad. Violet Sigerson died last week, a natural death, of pneumonia. I was the attending physician. Though she and Irene renewed their friendship, Violet remained an inmate of St. Giles, saying it was her home. I understood that decision: though changes have occurred in my own life, I have decided to stay at 221B. But life has changed for me. In these past months, we all went out together, often. Dined at Simpson's, watched children ice skating on the Serpentine.

I asked her at that time if she would like to meet Mycroft, who, after all, was also her half-brother. She told me that she had, in fact, met Mycroft in the past and that she did not care to renew his acquaintance. She asked me if I feared Mycroft's wrath in publishing her story, and I replied that I did not. She never explained under what circumstances she had encountered Mycroft.

When she was dying, Violet told me that she had kept a journal years ago. "You have written very well, very truthfully, about Sherlock and me," she said. "But I have saved a scrap, Dr. Watson, of my own writing. The rest of my journal I burned. There's no use looking for it. But this scrap." Her voice was low, she rested between sentences. "I should like to let people know of . . . of my love for him—how it was for me. Knowing him, merely knowing my brother, gave me incomparable happiness."

I nodded.

"Would you print my scrap as a postscript to your book?"

Afterword

February 1, 1888

The Library
St. Giles Hospital, London

   *The carpet is clean. You are not in the carpet
but, Sherlock, I see it through your eyes. I look
into its oatmeal fiber, its nubby tucked-in
herringbone, and think "Sherlock" and feel joy.*

   *I want to take in the world because you live in
it. It started with breathing, when I came back
here to London, from the Continent. Suddenly the
air was joy in my nostrils. You lived. You were
healing. Then my ears were double—yours and
mine. I couldn't tell if yours were in mine, or
mine in yours.*

   *In Munich, we wanted Mozart—the "Sinfonia
Concertante" for violin and viola. You said, "If
only there were a means, Violet, whereby you
could play both parts." I replied, "Time that is
serial cannot be made simultaneous." And our
little companion, Albert, told us that time was not
what we thought it was. He was so droll, surely
the child of our minds, if not our bodies. He
pronounced the "Sinfonia" to be the most perfect
of Mozart's violin music.*

   *Now I want piano music—Chopin, both hands
full of notes, rolling waves of opulent sound—the
"Ocean" étude, the études named "Winter Wind"
and "Revolutionary." There should be one named
"Rebirth" for you.*

— 221 —

The winter wind howls now beyond the barred glass window of this library. Baker Street lies to the north, and I look that way through the blackness. Here there is gentle lamplight, and in your room, you sit in lamplight. You think of something that amuses you, and I smile. We are connected, though to you I have slipped into memory. Let me be remembered only this way—as one who truly loved you.

This morning when I woke up alone in my small cell, sunshine was in my eyes. I sat up in bed, fingered the lawn of my nightgown, and looked at the great beauty filling the room. This is what it is to love, I thought. To have someone. Though to have you is only to have you in my thoughts. Yet, you do exist! Someplace the sunlight falls on your face.

Sometimes imagination fails me: the world is no longer continuous, and we are not connected. A great black cap of depression sits first on my forehead, then covers my face, my body. I know that as the years wear on, I may live in perpetual darkness. The morning sun may lose its power.

I believe men and women were meant to be companions. I was meant to use my gift, to live recognized, even honoured, for my music. I have no companion, no acknowledgement. But you would never have known peace as long as you thought me alive. The black cap is always waiting for me: "Deny yourself and enter into darkness" is the banner twisted around it.

I would advise all women to run from such a decision as I have made for your dear sake. But it was my nature to make it. And I am a human being as well as a woman.

Sometimes I think of the forbidden, the impossible. My body thinks of it. My body wants . . . But that way, real madness lies. And sooner than it need be.

Now is a heightened dance of the senses. What my eye falls on, I love to see. What the ear hears is thick with joy. Because we have been known to each other, I live in this moment as I did not before: loving the texture of the carpet, the glowing globe of the lamp and its light falling on my moving hand.

Just now I threw down the pen, left the little desk, paced over the carpet whose simple cleanliness caused me to take note and rejoice. My skirt lapped at my ankles. I am so alive and so in need of you, Sherlock. I want to bite the air. I want to pull the books off the shelves with my teeth. Where is the peace in sacrifice?

Did my mother's blood rage like this when she went to her forbidden lover? My mother, whom I curse and bless. She has given me the mirror of my soul, my brother, my darling. And she has made the completion of my happiness impossible.

I will never leave this place. I swear it. I will never intrude on whatever life you have made for yourself. But, is our problem—our case—really

*beyond our solving? Sherlock, could you not come
for me? Let us think together, once more.*

So I have included Violet's words from the library, St.
Giles Hospital for the Insane.

I have just now transcribed them.

My page grows brighter, and I look up to see Irene
holding a lamp in her hand. She smiles at me, and I know
that she is telling me to come to bed. Many a night, she has
thus come to guide me from my writing to my rest, for we
are married now.

"One moment, more, my dear," I say.

I wish to record the dream I had last night.

I dreamt that I was ascending familiar stairs to these old
rooms on Baker Street, and yet the place was not familiar:
it seemed to grow larger. It seemed that I was in the palace
of a king. At last I reached an upper floor and threw open
the door to what I thought would be familiar rooms. But
instead, a lake spread before me. A vast and frozen lake,
outdoors. Near the shore where I stood, a swan boat was
frozen in the ice, and the swan's head seemed encased in
glittering ice. In the misty distance rose the white tower
and turrets of a ghostly castle.

I heard the sound of a skater stroking his way over the
ice, and then I saw that this skater was Sherlock Holmes.
He held out his hand as though to grasp the hand of
someone else, and it seemed in my dream that *I* held out
my hand to him. But he ignored me, standing on the
shore. He was glancing across the ice for another skater.

Then I saw her coming. She was dressed exactly like
Holmes himself, in an Inverness coat and deerstalker cap,

but I had no doubt, even at a distance, that this was his sister. She skated just as he had, fearlessly and gracefully, and like him, she seemed a cold figure and alone on the frozen lake. But she skated toward Sherlock.

She held out her hand to him—I saw that they both were young again—and hand-in-hand they skated away from me across the lake.

THE END

ABOUT THE AUTHOR

SENA JETER NASLUND grew up in Birmingham, Alabama, where she attended public schools and received the B.A. from Birmingham-Southern College. She has also lived in Louisiana, West Virginia, and California. She received the M.A. and Ph.D. degrees from the University of Iowa Writers' Workshop. She is the author of the national bestseller *Ahab's Wife* and the short-story collection *The Disobedience of Water*. Her short fiction has appeared in *The Paris Review*, *The Georgia Review*, *The Iowa Review*, *Michigan Quarterly Review*, and many other journals. For twelve years, she directed the Creative Writing Program at the University of Louisville, where she teaches and holds the title Distinguished Teaching Professor. Concurrently, she directs the low-residency M.F.A. in Writing Program at Spalding University, Louisville. She is coeditor of the literary magazine *The Literary Review* and the Fleur-de-Lis Press at Spalding University, and has taught at the University of Montana and Indiana University. A recipient of grants from the National Endowment for the Arts, the Kentucky Foundation for Women, and the Kentucky Arts Council, she lives in Louisville with her husband, John C. Morrison, an atomic physicist.

☖ Perennial

Books by Sena J. Naslund:

AHAB'S WIFE
ISBN 0-688-17785-9 (paperback)
Named 'One of the Best Novels of the Year' by *Time Magazine*
A *New York Times* Notable Book of the Year
National Bestseller

A breathtaking, magnificent, and uplifting story of one woman's spiritual journey, based on a passage from the great American novel *Moby Dick*. Naslund takes the story beyond tragedy to redemptive triumph in this evocative novel filled with humanity and wisdom, and rich in historical detail. Melville's spirit informs every page of her tour de force.

"Beautifully written. Lyrical . . . alluring and wise."—*Los Angeles Times*

THE DISOBEDIENCE OF WATER
Stories and Novellas
ISBN 0-688-17845-6 (paperback)

A collection of finely perceived, beautifully crafted stories evoking passion and heartbreak, intelligence and unapologetic humanity. While Naslund's characters accept that their inner tides cannot be brought into obedience, sometimes, in the act of recognizing the force of their own hopes, needs, and fears, they learn to navigate those waters.

"Naslund has an eye for odd, telling details and a gift for rendering (and respecting) this oddness in language."—*The New York Times Book Review*

SHERLOCK IN LOVE
ISBN 0-688-17844-8 (paperback)

A brilliant, thoroughly entertaining homage to the greatest detective that literature ever produced. Upon the death of Sherlock Holmes, the venerable Doctor Watson decides to write his old friend's biography. A string of questions relating to Sherlock's life begins to surface to which Watson must find the answers . . . and before the anonymous threats of his life become a reality.

Available wherever books are sold, or call 1-800-331-3761 to order.